AF366629

THE SECRETARY'S ASSETS

HENRY CONNERS

The Secretary's Assets
By Henry Conners
Copyright © 1981, 2024
Cover art by Fotor
ISBN print: 978-91-89822-62-7
ISBN e-book: 978-91-89822-63-4
Published by Yabot AB, Sweden, 2024

More SEX IN THE CITY

Available in print, as e-book & audiobook.

In the heart of bustling New York City lies the prestigious law firm of Moore, McKenna & Crane, where ambition knows no bounds.

Legal Partners delves into the high-stakes world of legal sex play, where aspiring lawyers will stop at nothing to claim the coveted partner's corner office.

Follow Jane's, a struggling secretary unable to retain a job. A sliver of hope arrives when she's offered a position with an agency veiled in enigmatic allure, offering services far beyond the realm of clerical duties.

In **The Secretary Position**, Jane finds herself entangled in a world of forbidden desires and unspoken fantasies.

Welcome to the wildest **Manhattan Rock Party**, where anything can happen.

As Jennifer Davis prepares to bid adieu to her college days, her parents are no-shows, leaving her feeling abandoned. Luckily, her former roommate Susan comes to the rescue with an invitation to a steamy party in the city that never sleeps.

CHAPTER ONE

Jessica Daniels stirred restlessly in bed and wondered what had awakened her. Soft, girlish laughter coming faintly from the living room of the big apartment gave her the answer. It was Saturday night, and her younger sister Amy had brought her date home for a little amusement and probably some sex.

Oh, damn, Jessica thought, wide awake now. I wish she had taken him to a motel. This is torture! I'll have to listen to her make out again.

Amy was eighteen and very popular. Some guy was always calling her. The men never asked for Jessica, though. She was just as attractive and sexy as Amy, but one awful reality kept her from having dates; she was nearly six feet tall.

Men liked to look at her, though. When she walked down the street, whether in short skirts or tailored pants, she could turn heads, like Amy. But her extreme height was good for only one thing so far. She was a private secretary for a large insurance firm in downtown New York, and she did a lot of modeling in her spare time.

Her very long legs, her high jutting breasts, and her facial beauty made her very much in demand.

Knowing her sister was having fun in the living room made sleep out of the question. She stretched, turned on a lamp at the head of the bed, and slid from between the sheets. She glanced in the vanity mirror and swore under her breath.

She almost hated her body, especially the long, light-brown

legs that stilted her so high. It seemed she was always looking down at others. Nature had played an awful trick on her. Her mother, Martha was only five-six, about Amy's height, but her deceased father had been six-two.

She tried not to remember all the agonizing years of growing up, when other girls had asked her how the weather was, "up there," her nickname of "Stilts." She tried to forget that she had never had a real date in her life. And now, at age twenty-one, she began to wonder whether she ever would.

She didn't count offers of a night out from a few older men she had met in her modeling. It was easy to see that such men considered her a kind of curiosity, and she had developed a thick skin for that kind of people. She had never yet met a man she would be willing to screw as badly as she needed it.

Basically, she was just as passionate as Amy or Martha. She simply had to find her own way of relieving her sexual tensions. From the age of eleven, when she had first discovered her clitoris until she had reached eighteen, she had used her hands. Oh, she still liked it with her fingers, but she had discovered that a vibrating dildo gave her more satisfaction.

If I ever find the right guy, I'll fuck him to death, she thought wistfully. But who wants a too-tall woman?

Another cozy laugh from the living room made her shiver.

Many times before, when Amy had brought a guy home for an evening of fun, Jessica had Iain in bed and let her imagination work while she played with her crotch and breasts, aching fiercely for a man's touches and attention. But tonight, she was going to do things a little differently and had decided to slip out into the hallway and take a few peeks.

Martha wouldn't be home until very late. She was out with her steady, a prominent attorney who had recently lost his wife. They usually went to his apartment for their sex pleasures after visiting some night spots. Jessica envied her mother, too. She knew how to wangle her steady stuff. She was still a very beautiful woman.

Jessica moved to her closet and found a light robe to cover her sheer red nightie. She turned off the lamp and slipped from her bedroom out into the nearly dark hallway. Amy giggled intimately, and the sound rasped Jessica's nerves. She felt wetness in her pussy. Her clit was rising.

The light increased in brightness as she slinked along the carpeted hallway until she could peer into the living room. A high planter near the end of the hall would let her peek without being seen.

Her first glimpse of Amy and her date, sitting side by side on the big sofa, sent shivers along her body. The sofa faced the hallway entrance, and Jessica had a fine view. They were kissing, and his hand was under Amy's miniskirt, his fingers pressing into a pair of lace-trimmed yellow panties.

Amy's left hand was on his basket, and he had a very big lump there. He was blond, and as their mouths parted, Jessica recognized him. He was John Castle. His father owned a big Ford reseller in downtown New York. John had recently been divorced by his society wife. Amy was a classy broad; she picked them wisely. She planned eventually to marry some wealthy man.

Jeff Daniels, Jessica's deceased father, had left Martha very well fixed. She owned some high-priced rentals, and the lavish apartment the mother and daughters lived in was one of them. While they didn't move in the top echelons of New York society, they weren't far below it. They were "in".

The kiss ended, and as he drew back, Jessica could see that the tip of Amy's frock was open, her fine full tits almost ready to fall out. His hand stayed between her long, smoky thighs, which were sleekly nyloned. She raised her crotch against his playing fingers. Her hand continued to roam across his big basket.

She laughed cozily again. "Let's take off some clothes, huh?"

He nodded and whispered something in her ear, and she giggled. Her tongue wiggled out from between her thick, sensual lips. His mouth returned. She began to open his trousers. His fingers began to slip inside the yellow panties. Her thighs spread farther apart.

Jessica trembled again, a sweet urgency building in her loins. Peeping was murder! She had never watched anyone screwing, although she had listened plenty of times. In her younger years, she had heard Jeff bouncing Martha. Her muffled moans and cries of delight, the soft sighing of the bed in the master bedroom at their former home in South New York, had made Jessica quiver with envy.

They had made it last a long, long time. Invariably, Martha had had several climaxes before Jeff made it. In the mornings after, Martha would look so pleased with herself. Obviously, she had been a good piece of ass then and probably still was. Jeff had been much older than Martha.

Well, Martha was a very wonderful person, always generous

and friendly. She had insisted that both daughters go on the pill so there wouldn't be any messes.

The only trouble was that Jessica had never been able to test the pill's effectiveness. Although she had read the right books and looked at pictures of naked men, she had never seen a rigid cock, let alone held one in her hand or taken one in her cunny.

The thought that she might never do all of those delicious, sexy things was almost frightening.

Of course, she knew she could easily hook up some older man or go down to a joint and pick up somebody, but she wasn't that desperate yet. Perhaps if she went to some larger city or a swinging spot like Las Vegas, she could find what she was looking for. Her mirror told her she was a very classy number it was simply that her height scared off the guys who appealed to her.

She slipped her right hand inside the thin wrapper and under the hem of her nightie. Her pussy was wet and swollen, her prominent clitoris ached for knowing teases and touches, and her nipples were stiff as finger-ends. It hurt her to realize that Amy and Martha knew she played with herself, but of course, smart girls did, and she would never forget the time she had watched her mother sprawled out on her bed, using a dildo.

That exciting performance had started her thinking about an artificial penis of her own. Well, she had been using hers for several years. She was almost sick of it. She needed the real thing, the feel of a man, the sweet touch of a real cock entering her untouched pussy.

Recently, another thing had been bugging her. Her only fairly close girlfriend, Alexa Daniels, a beautiful young model Jessica worked with now and then on assignments, had slyly indicated that she wanted to make it with Jessica. Alexa had experienced some kind of bad scene with a guy a few years before, and she wanted to try some girl-girl sex.

Jessica was tempted. She knew a lot of it was going on. Two girls in the office where she worked were having an affair. They didn't look butchy, both were quite feminine and attractive. She found some girls interesting. She realized that if she did go for it, she would be the leader, the aggressor. But men interested her much more, even though she might feel more at ease with another woman.

No, that route was out.

New action on the sofa scattered her thoughts. She felt a sweet, hot thrill in her pussy. Amy was getting her hand inside John's pants, her curvy ass moving on the sofa cushion. His hand inside her panties was making her thighs quiver.

Oh, damn! Jessica thought. If only some handsome guy would do that for me. A few soul kisses and touches like that, and I'd blow my stack for sure. Why the hell don't they take their clothes off and screw?

Jessica knew her younger sister was passionate enough. They had adjoining bedrooms and a connecting bathroom, and several times recently, Jessica had heard Amy huffing and puffing in the toilet while she used her hands on her body.

Martha had her own dildo. She had mentioned it to Jessica, but evidently, Amy hadn't bought herself one yet. She dated enough so that she didn't need an artificial penis. The real thing was obviously much more fun.

Suddenly Amy succeeded in bringing John's cock out in sight. Jessica trembled, and her pussy leaked more juice. It was so deliciously sex, so hard and swollen, Jessica almost cried out. It looked at least seven inches long. The circumcised knob was wet and purplish.

Their kiss ended, and Amy giggled. She breathed something in his ear, her fingers playing gently on his cock.

"Right, baby," he muttered. His hand in her panties moved faster. She urged her hips higher. Her right arm tightened around his neck. She lifted her left hand from his rigid prick and opened the top of her frock. Her titties emerged, the dark nipples very stiff. His head lowered to them.

The motion of his hand indicated he had a finger in her cunny. Amy's pretty face began to twist, her head went back, her thighs quivered, her ass went up and down. Her heavy, uneven breathing was a dagger in Jessica's senses. Amy's right hand returned to his penis, but she didn't pump it.

Her thick, sensual lips drew back, her pearl-white teeth showed, and her breasts arched out farther. A low, fierce whine broke from her throat. She was almost ready to have a climax.

God, this is torture! Jessica thought, pressing her cunny very hard. I shouldn't be here peeping. I'm awful. I'm dirty. A man and a girl having fun deserve to be alone.

Suddenly Amy's body stiffened, she uttered a sharp cry of delight, and her rounded ass jerked swiftly up and down. She was getting her goodies. The agonized expression on Amy's face turned into a wide smile of triumph. She softened and wound both arms around his neck, humping slowly on his hand.

"Ohh, that was good, honey!" she giggled.

He kissed one of her nipples, his hand staying in her lacy yellow panties. He murmured in her ear. She nodded eagerly.

Jessica was frantic. Her swollen clit ached, her breasts ached, and more wetness oozed from her cunny. She leaned her left shoulder against the wall, pressed a finger on each side of her clitoris, and began to draw the honey from her loins. She simply had to finish!

Seeing a swollen cock for the first time was simply too exciting. The whole sexy scene was just horribly fascinating. Amy has asked him to play her into an orgasm, and now they would take off their clothes, and he would have his fun.

Jessica felt stinging, burning thrills shoot up her long thighs. Her ass curved out, and she opened her legs. The first sweet pounds of her erotic sensation nearly made her shout! Honey pulsed from her clit, her nipples hardened, and for breathless heartbeats, she was lost in her shivery thrall. It was the strongest climax she had enjoyed for days and days. It was pounding through her crotch.

When she opened her eyes, she saw Amy removing her frock, lifting it over her long, dark tresses. John had his shirt off, revealing his tanned chest. His eyes were glued to Amy's figure. In nylons and yellow panties, she did look voluptuous. She hadn't worn a bra her stand-out titties were so firm she certainly didn't need one.

As the yellow bikini briefs came down, Jessica had her first look at her sister's fun-ready pussy. She had hardly any pubic hair, a characteristic that ran in the family. Her cunny lips were all swollen, the wetness between them glistening in the dim light.

But the feature attraction was John's naked body, his seven inches angling stiffly out from his thatch of blond hair, his good-sized nuts. Jessica gripped her drippy cunt and shuddered with terrible envy.

"You sure we're alone here, baby?" John asked, moving toward Amy.

"Sure, honey," she said, sticking her tongue out. "Mom's out on a date, and Jessica went to a late movie. Relax."

Oh, that damned liar, Jessica thought. I believe she brought him here on purpose, just to torment me. Oh, hell! I have to have another cum. I'm dying for prick!

"Let's find a bedroom," John muttered. He moved up close to Amy, his cock flattened against her belly. She coiled her arms around his neck, pushed her titties into his chest, and tipped her head for another kiss.

If only I could look up at some handsome guy, Jessica thought, biting her lower lip. I'm always looking down at somebody.

"I like it right out here, honey," Amy giggled, squirming her pretty ass. She still wore her heels and nylons.

He nodded and took Amy's mouth. Jessica caught a flash of his tongue before their lips met. Amy's hungry moan indicated just how much she enjoyed a deep French kiss. His hands slipped down her waist to her rump, his fingers pressed and kneaded. Her thighs began to spread. She hunched at his groin. She arched her tits more firmly into his torso.

The kiss went on and on until Jessica could hardly bear watching. Again, she began to play with her tumid, achy clitoris. Her left hand rose to her breasts. She opened the thin wrapper, sliding her fingers in on a pointy, swollen tittie. Ohhh, her mounds were really out there tonight. When she was really turned on, they expanded measurably. Her nipples were very stiff, almost as hard as her clit.

She decided she wouldn't climax so swiftly this time. As long as she had gone this far with her dirty peeping, she felt like enjoying it as much as possible. She had become very adept at drawing out her lonely fun, playing right up to a climax and then waiting.

Only one thing bothered her. If and when Amy went to the potty, she would have to enter the hallway where Jessica was standing. Well, Amy surely wouldn't use the facilities until she had enjoyed her screw...

The long kiss finally ended, and Amy whispered in his ear again. He nodded and chuckled. Amy drew away, took a pillow from the sofa, and tossed it on the floor. John sank down on his back, his head resting on the pillow, his wet-knobbed cock looking even larger than ever.

Oh, she's going to top him! Jessica thought, dizzy with need. I've heard a man can last longer that way. She wants to have as much fun as she can. And I get to see the whole sexy thing!

Amy sank down above her blond lover, her thighs straddling his groin, her torso angled over his chest. Her left thigh spoiled Jessica's view of his rigid cock, but the vision was exciting enough. His hands lifted to Amy's beautiful, jutting breasts, and he filled his palms with them. His wide smile, a faint flush on his face, told how enthused he was with his sexy date.

"You still going to take me up to the lake tomorrow, honey?" Amy cooed. Her ass began to wiggle. She didn't have his cock inside yet, though.

"Hell, yes, beautiful," he smiled. "A buddy of mine is up here from L.A. You think you could line up a date for him?"

"Sure thing," Amy giggled. "I think I know just the gal for him."

"Good. You really got a fine pair, baby."

Amy giggled, sticking her tongue out at him. "I love to have 'em played with, honey."

His fingers roamed across her swollen tits. He teased her tumid nipples. Amy shivered; her pretty ass moved back a little, then forward. She was sliding her pussy on his slanted cock.

They were so casual about it! Jessica was sure she wouldn't be able to talk with a stiff prick so close to her cunny. But she was learning her younger sister was showing her a few intimate tricks.

She pressed her palm hard on her mons, feeling pussy wetness seep out on her fingers. Her clit was ready to pulse again, her whole crotch flamed, and she couldn't delay her climax much longer.

A quick squirm of Amy's rump, a gasp of pleasure from her lips, and a slow lowering of her hips told what was happening. She was taking his prick, at last!

"Jesus, that's good!" he muttered.

"Nnnnnnn!" Amy breathed. "You know it!"

Slowly, she began to fuck. Her thighs slid forward, hugging his sides. She straightened, sitting upright, her light brown ass moving back and forth. She had it all! His hands stayed on her puffy tits, and she gripped his extended arms. She hunched three times and rested.

John groaned with pleasure. Amy's jerky breathing, the quiver of her thighs, and her look of intense thrall made Jessica so wildly envious she nearly cried out. It was agony watching her sister screw! It was just too much!

She wanted to slip back toward her bedroom, but her feet seemed rooted to the floor. She couldn't remember when she had been so furiously turned on, so hungry for a man. The awful need in her crotch was like a dagger. She couldn't play with her passion any longer, she had to cum!

Shuddering, she opened her thighs farther and slipped her middle finger into her pussy, keeping her thumb on her tensing clitoris. She wished she had brought her dildo from its hiding place in the bedroom, but she didn't want to leave and get it right now she had to see the finish.

Amy hunched again, very slowly. Her grip on his arms tightened, her head turning back. John didn't seem too excited yet. He was letting Amy gauge her own passion, letting her play with her needs. Jessica remembered vividly how her father and mother had made a screw last and last, the measured sighs of the bed, the long pauses between humps.

Martha had invariably climaxed several times during an hour-long screw. Her muffled cries of delight, a faster creaking of the bedsprings, had made Jessica horribly envious. But the very best and most exciting sounds had come through the dividing wall when Jeff finally made it. His loud groans and Martha's shouts, a dramatic jiggling of the whole bedframe, indicated they were finishing together. Jessica had always had several finger orgasms while her parents had enjoyed their sex.

Well, Martha was probably having fun at her boyfriend's place right now. Amy was having hers, too...

The action on the living room floor suddenly quickened, sucking Jessica back to the vivid present. Amy's ass moved faster. She wasn't pausing now; she was staring into her short strokes!

"Yes, ohhh!" Amy cried fiercely. Her tawny rump was a blur of movements, her head swung way back, and her white teeth showed again. John's face contorted, too. His hips lifted, he clutched at Amy's swollen tits, he groaned loudly. His legs kicked the carpet.

Suddenly, they were both thrusting and straining together. He was shooting his jism, and Amy was cumming around his prick! Her last swift, hard dramatic hunches, a shake of her whole body, told how beautifully she was reacting to a spraying cock!

Their mingled exclamations of erotic delight brought Jessica's need to a violent culmination. Her clitoris pulsed, her hips wiggled, her tits pushed way out. The honeyed throbs of her joy had never been sweeter! She was cumming really hard! For pounding golden seconds, she was utterly lost in her culmination.

She staggered and sank to the floor.

CHAPTER TWO

Amy felt the last delicious throbs of John's cock in her twitching pussy, savoring the glorious thrills of relief that washed through her crotch. Getting a handsome man's squirts of jism was really where it was at. His seven-incher reached just far enough in her snug, slick cunny. She had hoped he wouldn't cum so soon, but he was strong, and virile he would surely be good enough for at least one more burst of cockjuice.

His hands fell from her swollen titties. She softened and cuddled down on him, squeezing him with her thighs and arms and cunny. Wonderful, simply wonderful! She hadn't had a good screw since the Saturday before, and her date had fizzled out much too quickly.

She had been after John Castle for a long time. She had seen him around town, she had noticed his glances at her, and on the past Wednesday afternoon, she had put on her shortest miniskirt and tightest sweater and wiggled into the Ford showroom where she knew he was sales manager of his father's agency.

Luckily, John had spotted her and waved aside the salesman who had stepped up to wait on her, and she had started into her wide-eyed, innocent ploy that had always worked before. He had shown her several new cars, and when she moved in under the steering wheel, she had let him get a good look between her thighs. He had asked her for a date, and the whole thing had turned out beautifully. He had taken her to the Tapadera Lounge, one of New York's finest, they had danced and had several drinks, and now she had what a hot, sexy girl needed pussy full of cock.

He was unattached, he made good money, and he might just be the guy she was looking for...

While she rested, she sneaked a glance over at the shadowy hallway. Jessica wasn't in sight now, but she had been peeking earlier. The poor girl!

I really shouldn't bring guys here to the apartment when Jessica is home, Amy thought guiltily. It just makes her all the more desperate for a man of her own. I always was a kind of show-off, though. If Jessica wasn't so backward and shy and spooked about her tallness, she could be getting her regular prick, too. She's a very classy dish, and so am I.

She felt his cock lose some of its hardness, and she jazzed her ass a few more times. The slick, gooey connection, pussy juice, and jism leaking down around his nuts gave her a delicious sensation of closeness and intimacy.

"Jesus, that's good, baby," he muttered, caressing her waist and ass.

"Oh, right on," she breathed, sliding her tits back and forth on his chest. "There's a lot more where that came from, honey."

He chuckled. Another thing she liked about him was his sense of humor. He didn't get all uptight about a screw. She could tell already he was going for seconds and maybe thirds. Wonderful!

Jessica, back in her bedroom under the covers, stretched her long legs and sighed. Her needs were relieved for the moment; she had stuffed some tissues between her thighs to catch her drippage.

A light was on in the connecting bathroom. She heard her sister in there cleaning up after her screw. The light stayed on, and a moment later, she heard a cozy girlish laugh, and then John was using the facilities. The toilet flushed, and the light went out. They would probably get in Amy's bed and enjoy more playing around and more fucking.

I almost hate her, Jessica thought, shivering. She knew I'd listen in. I think she saw me peeping, too. Ohhh, hell!

She remembered a story she had read about twin sisters trading places in bed with a date. Well, that was out. Amy wouldn't share a handsome stud like John, even if they could make the switch. John might like a new pussy, though.

A conversation she had had with her mother a few days before ran through her mind...

"Jessica, you ought to circulate more," Martha said. "Haven't you run into some interesting guys at the office?"

"No," Jessica answered.

"I don't think you try very hard, honey. I saw a beautiful tall girl with an average-sized man the other day." She laughed. "You have a lot going for you. Pretty ass and long legs and nice titties."

"I guess I'll end up being an old maid," Jessica said dully.

"Oh, hell. Maybe you expect too much, honey. I've seen the way Alexa Daniels acts around you. Are you two screwing?"

"No!" Jessica objected. Although she was used to frank words from her mother, the idea of a Lesbian thing made her cheeks hot.

"Good," Martha smiled. "Keep looking, honey." Her voice lowered. "But don't get too involved with that dildo..."

* * *

A noise drew her back to the vivid present.

Jessica trembled, hearing suggestive sounds from Amy's bedroom. She and John were in there, all right. Sure, Martha knew Jessica had an artificial cock Martha had one, too. There weren't many secrets between the mother and her daughters.

An excited giggle from Amy and a laugh from John, coming very clearly, made Jessica realize that Amy had left her bathroom door open. She had done it on purpose so Jessica could hear every word and sound. This was going to be almost as bad as watching them make out.

Jessica swore under her breath, slid from her bed, and moved in the darkness to her vanity. She opened the lower right drawer and drew out her imitation penis. Her need was rising again. She had to have at least one more big orgasm. She returned to the bed, drew the covers over her, and tossed the pussy-wet tissue on the floor. She eased her sensitive tits out of her nightie and began to stroke them. She kept the dildo between her thighs to warm it. Sometimes, she ran hot water over it, but that was out tonight.

"Ohhh!" came dramatically from Amy's bedroom. Amy, of course. "Love that finger!"

John laughed again. The thought of Amy getting finger-played was excruciatingly awful. And before long, he would have his cock in her again. Damn, damn.

Jessica kept her left hand on her swollen tits and gripped

the dildo in her right hand. She opened her long shanks, curved her crotch upward, and began to ease the head of the plastic prick into her shivery pussy. Oh, it felt good! Her fingers never reached in far enough. Of course, the center of her fun was her clit, but having something inside made the sensations much sweeter. Gripping the handle firmly, she slid the seven-inch shaft deeper and began to pump it.

I hate myself when I do this, she thought. But as long as I've started, I'm going to enjoy every second of it. Mmmmmmm! The feeling is really sharp tonight. I guess it's because I saw a stiff cock and saw Amy taking it. Damn! I am going to do something about finding a date. The next time some guy wants to take me out, I'm going. I can't be so fussy. I need a man between my legs. Ohhhh, damn!

Sometimes, she imagined a composite image of her ideal lover, a blend of Wilt Chamberlain and Paul Newman, but it was all so impossible. Like Amy, she wanted to marry a strong and virile guy who would be after her pussy all the time.

She stroked the dildo three times and rested, enjoying the shivers of increasing pleasure. She traveled her fingers across her expanded titties, feeling the peaks stiffen. They were growing more sensitive every day. Her nipples were much longer when she was sexually excited. All the photographers she worked with on modeling assignments liked the way her tits jutted, giving the frocks and undies an added attractiveness.

But her long legs were what they photographed most. Her last job had been modeling bikinis. She did look very good in them. The studio owner had asked her about modeling in some nudie sequences, and she had said she would think about it.

He had connections with one of the large-circulation girlie magazines. She wasn't sure she wanted to see herself erotically posed in some centerfold. She really didn't need the money.

An excited giggle from Amy sent her thoughts flying. The bed wasn't creaking, yet they were still playing around.

Jessica trembled with envy and stroked her plastic prick again. The sweet ache in her crotch was almost unbearable she couldn't hold off much longer. Juice was running from her cunny down on the sheet, and she didn't care. It had happened before. Martha had kidded her about the tell-tale stains. Oh, just a few more plunges, and she would have her cum.

"Ohhhh, love that tongue, honey!" came startlingly from Amy's bedroom.

Jessica clenched her teeth. Her long thighs began to quake. John was eating Amy!

That was another deliciously intimate thing Jessica wanted in the worst possible way, a man's tongue sliding in her pussy. The way she was going, she might never have it, though; she did have to lose some of her shyness, her inhibitions. Other tails girls had fun. She was missing out.

A faint, low whine of delight reached Jessica's ears. Amy's bed commenced to creak. He had his prick in her again...

Amy adjusted the pillow under her ass and pulled her thighs forward. The dim bedroom light revealed John's handsome face, very flushed, the curve of his body as he started to screw. He knew how, all right. In hard and out slowly, three or four jabs, and then a pause. He hadn't tongue-dived her to a climax, but cock was better. She sure was ready for it!

"Man, that's good pussy," he muttered, his head lowering

to her swollen breasts. His lips found a tumid nipple, and he sucked it into his mouth.

"Oh, I love the way you screw, honey," she breathed. She tightened her vagina, and he shivered.

Amy remembered some of the things Martha had told her about pleasing a man, and they sure paid nice dividends! Clenching the vaginal membranes was one of the ploys; arching the tits up was another.

"Even if your date isn't a superman, you gotta come on strong," Martha had said. "You practice tightening your pussy, and you'll see how much they love it."

Martha was just a wonderful person. She wanted her daughters to enjoy life, and nothing was more enjoyable than screwing!

John shivered and stroked again, again, again. The luscious slide of cock in her twitching cunny, and the feel of his lips on her tender, tumid nipple sent dreamy thrills across her pelvis and out to the point of her clitoris. She was almost ready to cum!

"Oh, I'm gonna break one, honey!" she panted. "Please hold yours back, huh?"

He nodded, resting. His big nuts were bedded against her swollen, wet labia, his knob resting right at the door of her womb. Shuddering, she tightened her vagina again, then gave a little eager hunch, and that did it!

The sharp, honeyed jolts of her passion shot along her legs. Her nipples peaked high. Her clit began to pulse and cum! Her thighs jerked against his arched body. She heard herself crying out, and then the heaven beat through her pelvis. He started to poke, and she gripped his hips, holding him still while the waves of exquisite delight wrenched her crotch. Ohhh, this was what screwing was all about, cumming on a big hard prick!

She squealed!

* * *

Jessica heard her sister's cry of total ecstasy, and the hard, heavy beats of her own climax almost made her shout. The swift slide of the dildo in her drippy pussy, the heavenly twitches of her vagina, and the tensing of her clitoris swept her into dreamland. For long, shivery seconds, she floated in exotic thrall, her long legs shaking, her breasts heaving. It was one of the very best climaxes she had ever enjoyed!

As she tasted the wonderful washes of relief, as she softened and let the sensations feed her hunger, the full significance of her act hit her harder than it ever had before.

No matter how good it is, it's still dirty and awful, she thought. Martha told me not to get hung up on this artificial cock, and that's just what I'm doing. Ohhh, hell! I'm going to find a man somehow, somewhere.

She bit her lip, and tears of frustration wet her eyes. She yanked the dildo from her cunny and threw it across the room. Rolling over, she buried her face in the pillow, hating the sounds that came from her sister's bedroom.

* * *

Martha Daniels moved ahead of her date into the plush motel suite he had just rented for an evening of pleasure. She was very proud and excited. She had told her steady she was not in the mood for fun, which was a big fat lie. She had never been more ready for a hot, sliding prick.

Oscar Stern had finally asked her for a date. That he was Jessica's employer, owner of the big Stern insurance firm, didn't bother her one bit. That he was married didn't either. Sometimes, the married ones were the best.

Earlier, he had taken her to a small cocktail lounge north of the city, where he wouldn't be spotted by some inquisitive gossip. They had danced and had several drinks apiece, and now it was time for the nitty-gritty.

She remembered vividly the day she had walked into Oscar's office to see Jessica, his wide smile of appreciation as his dark eyes had slipped along her body. A very pretty black girl acted as his receptionist, and Jessica was his secretary.

Oscar closed and locked the motel unit door and slid his arms around Martha's waist. She held her head up and snuggled her prominent, thinly sheathed tits into his chest. Oh, it was good to be with a new man! She was getting marvelous vibes from him.

"I've been looking forward to this, Martha," he murmured. His right hand slipped down to her ass.

"Me, too, honey," she breathed. She pushed her crotch at his basket, and shivers of sweet anticipation stiffened her clitoris. "I'm flattered you called me, with all that nice, sexy young stuff in your office."

He laughed. "Too dangerous, Martha. Most of them have steadies, anyway. Except Jessica."

"I know," Martha said. "I wish she did have a guy. I'm sure she could give some man a real hot tussle."

His arms tightened. "I'll bet her mother is better."

"There's only one way to find out, honey," she breathed, opening her lips.

He trembled; his mouth came down on hers, and his tongue bored inward. She opened for his strokings, the sweet warmth of her need fanning out from her pussy. It was already wet. She pushed her crotch in harder, a hungry moan climbing in her throat. She hoped he wasn't too fast on the trigger. He was past fifty, and one good shot might be all he could muster.

Martha's steady was losing his grip. She hadn't had a screw since the previous weekend, and she had been forced to fill in with her trusty vibrating dildo. Poor Jessica was using hers much too much. It was just a shame she couldn't let go a little and have some fun with a man.

Oscar began to lift her frock in the back, and he soon had his fingers on her thinly pantied ass. Oh, it was wonderful to be wanted. She was so thankful she still had her figure. The dieting and exercises she put up with were more than worth it. Her ass was still round and firm, her legs were the legs of a woman half her age, and her tits didn't sag.

She was really getting into her best years. Her needs were increasing instead of diminishing. Maybe what she needed was a good young stud. Although she hadn't been part of the singles' society since she married Jeff, she knew how things operated in New York's nightlife. Young, clean studs were available, and she could easily afford them. But she liked to become a little involved with her boyfriends. She had grown to prefer older men. They seemed to appreciate her passion. And she had been thinking about getting into Oscar Stern's pants for a long time.

The way his tongue moved in her mouth, she had an idea he would like to eat pussy. She hoped so. It was one of her very favorite things.

Shivering, her cunny already swelling, she moved her tongue across his. His hands tightened on her ass, and she could feel the growing lump of his cock. It felt deliciously large. The first time she had seen him on the street, she had noticed the size of his basket the new styles in men's clothes were very revealing.

His mouth lifted, and he chuckled. "Very good, Martha."

"You ain't seen nothin' yet, big man," she cooed throatily.

He laughed. He wasn't going to get real heavy with it, and that pleased her, too. Obviously, this wasn't the first time he had chipped on his wife. He stood away and took off his jacket, his eyes boring at the twin juts of her breasts. She curved them out and weaved her shoulders.

"Mmmmm!" he said admiringly.

He was a tit-lover, too. Her frock was scooped low in front to display her two points of interest. At the cocktail lounge, he had admired them, and she'd shivered with delicious anticipation. Her nipples were stiffening in her thin, decorative bra.

He reached for her, and she backed away, laughing. "Just a minute, and I'll have 'em out so you can play with me, huh?"

He nodded and began to unbutton his shirt. She caught the zipper at her waist, her fingers shaky. The thrill of dating a new guy never diminished. Her whole crotch ached, and her panties were turning very wet.

A moment later, she was wearing only her bra and panties, and he was down to his briefs. The ridge of his prick, rising almost to the band of his shorts, gave her own eyes something to feast on. He caught her around the waist and drew her down on the edge of the bed at his left. Only one lamp burned, but it gave out enough light.

His left arm circled her shoulders, and his right went to her swollen breasts. Her undies were pale pink with white lace trim. She knew they looked sexy against her dusky figure. The drinks she had taken, the cozy atmosphere, and his fingers cupping a tit sent another sweet shiver along her body.

"Beautiful," he breathed, filling his hand with a breast-cone.

"I just knew you'd have good hands, honey," she giggled. "It unfastens in front."

She knew he'd give her a good playing. She just knew he was a gentleman. She hated a rush job. If he was good, she'd let him date her again.

His fingers found the key to her bra. The scented pink cups fell apart, and her bare, firmed breasts arched forward. Her inch-long dark nipples tingled delectably as he teased one and then the other.

"Ohhhh!" she breathed.

His head turned. He wanted her mouth again. Wonderful! She opened her lips and met his tongue with hers, coiling it over and under. She spread her thighs and pushed her crotch upward. His shiver of pleasure encouraged her, and she dropped her right hand on his cock-lump and caressed the hard manhood. Ohhh, he was well-hung, all right.

This is what a hot woman lives for, she thought. A nice slow buildup and then a nice long fuck. Damn! I hope he can last and last! I need about ten good, hard orgasms! I've been saving it up ever since he called.

His tongue stabbed deeper, his hand pressing hard into her left tit. She moaned and wiggled her ass, rubbing her thigh against his left leg. His man-aroma was driving her wild. She had to move when she was turned on. The men loved it.

Their mouths swerved apart, and she panted against his throat. He trembled as his hand dropped between her thighs, stroking the tender inner zones near her hungry pussy. She half-turned, urging her tits into his chest. She squeezed the covered ridge of his cock.

"Oh, get that big thing in me, honey!" she whispered.

He gave her cunny a lingering caress and stood up. He lowered his briefs, and she quickly skinned her pink, wet-crotched panties from her ass and along her legs. She crawled to the center of the bed, drawing her thighs far apart, curving her cunt.

He muttered thickly under his breath and swept over between her thighs. The touch of his big cock on her eager crotch whirled her thoughts. The view of his shaft, the swell of his knob so close to her cunny, sucked a moan from her throat. Sweet Jesus. He had a big one! Seven inches long and really thick. He still had his foreskin. The swollen glans framed by taut flesh, wet and ready for pussy, brought her crotch to the right angle.

Bringing his knees forward, he touched his cockhead to her expanded labia. She moaned and lifted her ass, snugging his hot knob against the door of her eager cunt. The sweet yield of her moistened flesh around his sex made her cry out with joy.

"Ohhh, Oh!"

"Ughhhhh," he muttered, giving her a hunch.

The luscious penetration, the erotic slow filling of her famished pussy, jerked her thighs back even farther. As his knob struck her depths, her vagina twitched and tightened. He shuddered, his eyes glazed with wonder.

"Sonofabitch!" he gasped.

"Oh, it loves what you've got, honey!" she panted.

His head lowered, his lips opened, and he took a tingling nipple in his mouth. She loved the way he was doing it, letting his cock soak a little before the strokes. He pushed in again, sounding the opening of her womb. Her vagina clenched, her clit erected against his cockshaft, and she felt the first heavenly twinges of her cum!

"Uhhhh!" she gasped. "Ohhhh, Jesus!"

Her breasts curved higher, her thighs jerked, her ass wiggled, and suddenly, the excruciating wait was over! She was getting her goodies! The sweet, quick churns of her pelvis, the exquisite clenchings of her cunt, hadn't been so deep and thorough for a long, long time. His cock was just thick enough to make her vagina respond the way she loved it, hard and sure!

He wasn't bucking and trying to shoot, either! He was letting her have her glory while he rested, his big cock jammed in tightly, his nuts caressing her swollen, juicy labia. The washes of relief were just delicious!

"Oh, honey!" she breathed, softening. "You sure got me off good!"

"Great, great!" he muttered. His cock tensed, and he drew it out.

She whimpered her disappointment, watching the pussy-wet shaft with hungry eyes. But he was right; if he kept it in her too long, he might blow his cum and then he might not be so hot for her pussy. She knew what happened to a man his age after he had his blast. He would start to cool and talk about splitting.

CHAPTER THREE

Alexa Daniels opened the door of her apartment and trembled as Jay Romero, her new boyfriend, took her around the waist and pulled her in close. Her shiver wasn't caused by sexual anticipation. It was more like revulsion. But she had a big plan, and she needed a guy like Jay to pull it off.

Although she had a beautiful body, long blonde hair, and model features, she didn't date many guys. She was much more at home with a girl. She was in between girlfriends, too. Her last steady, a cute brunette, had decided to stop the Lesbian affair and get married, the little bitch.

Well, it was fun to be seen out with a stud as good-looking and big as Jay. She could put up with a little straight sex if it got her what she wanted, and now Jay wanted what she had promised him by rubbing her pussy around on him at the Sahara Club.

She had spotted him two days before at a car wash place in Northtown. He was new in town. He really didn't have the look of a guy who had to wash autos for a living, but then he had a good sporty car of his own and money to spend, so maybe he was just temporarily down on his luck.

Her big plan had started forming the moment she had seen Jay.

"Nice layout, Alexa," he said, glancing around her apartment.

She giggled and curved her crotch at his big basket. She

wasn't going to tell him that unless she found some chick to share her bed and pay half the rent, she wouldn't be able to keep the apartment.

I wanted Jessica Daniels to move in with me, and the high-toned bitch wouldn't do it, she thought. She turned me down. And by God, I'm going to get even! I've been wanting to get in her panties for months!

"Want another drink before we start playing, honey?" she purred, snuggling her generous tits into Jay's chest.

"I'm okay, baby," he grinned. His dark eyes went to the V of her frock. It was shaped to accent the thrust of her tits. She was very proud of her knockers she had the best pair in the Oscar Stern Insurance office, and the best ass and legs, too. She loved to tease men with her figure.

She put on a good front where she worked. Jessica was the only girl there who knew she was Lesbian. The other chicks figured she was getting what most chicks wanted, a stiff, sliding prick. Well, she knew how to screw a man even though she hardly ever did. She would put out if it got her what she wanted, like a new dress, a trip to the beach, or a weekend in Vegas.

She had told Jessica she liked girls because some guy had given her a very rough time in her hometown in northern Washington, but it was a big fat lie. She had been interested in pussy since her junior high years, and she was sure she would never change.

"Well, let's sit down and be comfortable honey," she giggled, swinging away and twitching to the nearby sofa. She sat down and let the short hem of her frock slide back.

She wore long, dark nylons and black bikini panties. Blondes looked sexier in dark colors.

He was taking the bait, all right. He sat down at her right, his left arm sliding around her shoulders. Curving her titties out, she held her mouth up for a kiss. He smiled, his right hand went to her breasts, his head lowered. As their lips touched, his hand went inside her bra, and his fingers cradled a tit. Her thin bikini bra was strictly decoration; her boobs didn't need support. She squirmed and opened her mouth, feeling his tongue shoot inside. She closed her eyes and tried to imagine that Jessica was here instead of Jay.

No! Not Jessica. She hated that tall, snooty twat. Well, she could dream about that cocktail waitress at the Sahara, the one with the pretty narrow ass and pussy tits. The little pin on her uniform said her name was Carol. She would be worth a try.

Jay Romero enjoyed the firm resilience of Alexa's breast, the feel of her spreading lips, but it was very plain that she wasn't turning on. Her nipple wasn't hard; her actions all said put-on. Still, he was curious. At the car wash, she had given him the old come-on, and her sensational beauty had made his cock tingle.

He had seen quite a few very pretty mercenary young bitches like Alexa. He had even been married to one for less than a year. All show and no go-go.

Jay was from Los Angeles, a UCLA grad, and he was employed by a big insurance firm. He had come to New York on an undercover assignment to investigate the validity of a big payoff due to a certain fairly young widow whose doddering husband had supposedly fallen down some stairs and killed himself.

This kind of thing happened a lot. The police had found nothing amiss, a coroner's jury had called the death accidental, and the company he represented was going to have to come up with a couple of hundred thousand unless he could find something the cops hadn't.

The car wash job hadn't been necessary, but the widow he was investigating had her Jaguar cleaned there every few days, and it gave him a chance to look her over. The beneficiary was Melanie Welch, a not-bad brunette of around thirty. He had managed to keep her from getting a close look at him, though. One of these days, when he was ready, he would book a date with her. She might just let the cat out of the bag about her recently deceased husband.

Melanie had also inherited a big home and some rental income property. He didn't give a shit about that. It was his duty to try to save the insurance company that huge payoff.

Then Alexa Daniels had come in for a car cleaning, and she was after something, too. He had discovered where she worked and had learned that she usually went around with broads, not men. He wanted to see how far she would go to get whatever it was she wanted. It amused him to think she figured she had him completely hooked with her very good tits and ass and legs. Her mouth wasn't bad, either.

Maybe I can bang her pistol, for real, he thought, lifting a tit out of the fancy bra and teasing the flaccid nipple. It will be interesting, anyway. I haven't had a piece of ass since I left

Los Angeles. A new pussy is always interesting, even if she doesn't get her jollies.

He stroked his tongue in her mouth and felt her imitation shiver of excitement. Women were born actresses, and pretending to like sex was a thing broads had been doing for thousands of years. Trading pussy for the real things of life, like homes and luxuries, went on continually.

Breaking the kiss, he lifted her other breast out of her decolletage and began to work on it. The pink nipples were actually beginning to harden.

"Ohhh, nice," she whispered. She spread her thighs invitingly.

"Fine pair," he murmured.

"Like my thirty-eights, huh?" she giggled.

"That big, eh?" he chuckled. "No steady boyfriend, I take it."

"I told you I like to play the field," she breathed, watching his fingers. "Gals love variety, just like guys."

"Sure," he said. He reached down between her opened thighs and began to caress the inner planes of her nyloned thighs. She lifted her crotch and trembled again. He dropped his head to her tits and sucked a pink nipple inside. She ran her fingers through his hair and urged her titties out farther. He settled his hand on her pantied cunt. She trembled, giving a little uphunch.

"Groovy," she breathed. "You like that, too?"

He nodded and released the nipple, then moved his mouth to the other one. A definite stiffness was developing. Her tremor didn't seem all faked. He rolled his palm against her cunny in a way that most girls really went for. He had taken some pre-med, so he knew female anatomy very well and knew what made girls turn on, Lesbian or not. No matter how enjoyable a woman's body was in various areas, the clitoris was the trigger that fired the gun.

She closed her thighs and winced. "I'm a little tender there, honey. Don't you want to screw me now?"

He smiled to himself. "You've got such a beautiful figure. I want to really enjoy it."

She relaxed a little and let her legs re-open. He caressed her thighs, returning his mouth to a nipple. It was turning soft, but he sucked it back into rosy stiffness. She fondled his neck and wiggled a little, shivering again. With his lips, he brought her other nipple out. Her tits were firming, and her breathing was quickening. When he settled his palm back on her pussy curve, he felt wetness along her crevice.

A cock-teaser like her needed a good lesson. She was heating up in spite of herself.

"I gotta go to the can, honey," she murmured. "Why don't you get some clothes off, huh?"

He nodded and released her. She moved upright, and he watched the dainty flex of her ass, the sweet curves of her waist and thighs. Whatever her angle was, whatever she wanted, she was going to have to earn it.

* * *

Alexa closed the bathroom door, shivering. Things weren't going at all the way she'd expected the big bastard was dampening her cunny and making her clit ache. Her nipples tingled. She hadn't gone off with a guy since her junior high days before she discovered she liked pussy or knew what a pretty girl could do for her glands.

There was something definitely funny about Jay. He wasn't any car wash employee she could easily trick. His clothes were expensive, and his car was new. He was up to something underhanded, but she had no idea what it could be. He claimed he had just drifted into town looking for excitement.

I'll handle him, though, she thought, admiring her figure and looks in the bathroom mirror. I've used men before to get things I wanted. His cock will turn me off, but I'll get him off a couple of times, no matter how disagreeable it is, and then I'll tell him where he can get some good virgin pussy. I'm sure Jessica will go for him. Then, when she gets hung up good on him, I'll take him away from her. After all, I'm just about the best-looking twat in New York! No broad turns me down and gets away with it. I'll fix her ass, good!

She touched up her mouth, brushed her long blonde hair, and made herself very dainty again. She decided to leave her panties on. She looked sexier in them than out of them.

When she stepped out of the bathroom, he was undressed except for his briefs. The big lump inside them made her cringe.

"Let's go in the bedroom, honey," she giggled. She swayed her ass invitingly.

He grinned and followed her. She flicked on a bedside lamp and pulled the covers back, bending and curving her body in a way she knew would excite him. Yes, his cock was riding up inside his briefs, and it was so big she felt a little twinge of uncertainty. He was hung like a horse!

Posing prettily, she slipped her black lacy panties down from her butt, smoothed her smoky nylons high on her thighs, and spread herself out on the striped sheet. She angled her pussy up and weaved her ass. She had put a lot of lubricant in her vagina, so she felt sure his prick wouldn't hurt her.

As he slid his shorts down, she felt another shiver of revulsion. God! The knob was as big as a small apple, and the shaft was eight inches long!

* * *

Jay stood beside the bed and tensed his cock. He was proud of his sex tool. The size of it had scared a few chicks, and it was obviously scaring Alexa. Her exposed pussy, lightly sprinkled with blonde hair, brought some clear sap out on the uncircumcised knob. Her allure was good enough to stir his need, even though her cunny wasn't puffed with girlish excitement.

"Mmmm!" she giggled. "Some cock, honey."

Her nipples were flaccid again, he noticed. She must think he was pretty stupid.

"Say, you know something?" she added. "I'm acquainted with a girl who would really go for that."

He smiled. Maybe she was starting her ploy. "Oh, are you thinking about a threesome, baby?"

"Sure," she cooed.

He was sure that wasn't what she had in mind. "Who is this chick?"

"Jessica Daniels," Alexa said. "I work in the same office she does. A nice, tall, sexy brunette. You like dark gals?"

"I've heard they're pretty hot," he grinned, sliding down on the bed. He settled at her right, and she seemed a little surprised that he wasn't climbing between her thighs. "How come you're so cooperative?" he asked.

"Oh, you're new in town. I want to see you have some fun."

"Good," he grinned, sliding his right hand between her opened shanks. "Might be very interesting, a hot blonde like you and a brunette."

"You're a pretty special stud, you know," she breathed, arching her tits toward him and weaving her ass on the sheet. Her actions would have fooled almost any man; they had probably worked wonders before. She reminded him a little of a very beautiful hundred-dollar whore he had screwed in Las Vegas. But at least she had liked his prick and had blown her cookies three times in the two hours he had enjoyed with her.

But Alexa was a girl-lover. He had watched her at the nightclub; he had seen the interested little glances between Alexa and the classy cocktail waitress. Of course, some broads were AC-DC. They liked it both ways.

I'm. going to get her gun off, whether she wants it or not, he thought, settling his palm on her cunny.

He slid his play finger up and down her artificially lubricated crevice and found her clitoris. He leaned over her and took a pink nipple in his mouth. Her hands on his shoulders weren't very enthusiastic, but she was trying. He tickled her clit, and she shivered again, for real. The nipple began to rise. She tried to close her thighs again.

"Honey, get it in me, huh?" she breathed.

"Play with it a little and get it good and hard, baby, he said, watching her other nipple stiffen.

Her right hand reached for his prick, and her fingers went around it below the knob. He rolled her clit, and she grabbed his right wrist with her left hand, tugging.

"Honey, don't you want to screw now?" she giggled softly.

"Don't you like a finger cum?" he asked banteringly. He eased his finger into her pussy, and she shivered.

"Ohhhh, I love it inside better," she cooed.

Sure, he thought. Like a whore. He remembered the young prostitute in Los Angeles who had begged him not to play with her clit until she had an orgasm because it would lose her some business. The madam didn't want her girls cumming with the customers. She had given him a very fine mouth job, though, taking the load in her throat. She had saved herself from climax.

Well, Alexa wasn't a professional. Getting her off would give him a fine kick. Maybe she would like prick if she had the right man work on her body. Just maybe.

"Like this?" he murmured around Alexa's nipple, sliding his finger in and out of her lubricated pussy. It was average size, so he could get his cock inside with a little effort. Every time he stroked, he let his thumb push at her clit. It was swelling her shivers were for real.

She whimpered and clutched at his wrist again, closing her thighs.

"Please, honey!" she gasped. "Screw me!"

"I like to see how many times I can climax a sexy girl like

you, baby," he murmured. He stroked his finger faster, rolling her clitoris with practiced skill. The little nub was swelling, her thighs began to quake, and her nipple hardened. Her grip on his wrist relaxed, her legs opened wide, and her ass lifted in the old gesture of surrender.

* * *

Oh, damn him! Alexa thought, feeling the ripples of her excitement fan out from her tingling clit. The bastard is getting me off! Ohhh, shit! Here it comes, already. Oh, Oh, Oh!

The beats of delight that pulsed from her clit were so sharp and good she couldn't believe it! He knew just how to tease a clitoris and make it cum! Her legs were shaking, her ass lifting, her titties swelling. The throbs of delight lasted and lasted! She hadn't even had time to think about Carol, the sexy cocktail waitress.

* * *

Jay smiled as Alexa relaxed slowly, as her too-pretty face lost its strained expression. She had fought it, she had tried to keep from cumming, but he had brought her off anyway. The beautiful, clever bitch would get more orgasms, too, if she didn't get mad and ease him out. He had a good idea now of what she really wanted – setting him up with a broad she obviously hated, probably because she hadn't been able to make it with Jessica Daniels, whoever she was. His curiosity was stronger than ever.

"You cum pretty good, blondie," he chuckled, drawing his finger out of her cunny. He patted it and pressed it. Her hips lifted in an involuntary fuck-hunch. He could feel the waves of relief sweep her crotch and body. Her nipples were still hard, her tits still swollen.

"You're pretty good, honey," she giggled, opening her eyes. But it was phony; there was almost hatred in her voice in spite of her effort to be sophisticated about it.

He realized suddenly he didn't want to screw her. It would be phony, too. He could enjoy himself more by jacking off.

"What is it you're really after, Alexa?" he asked, rolling away and standing beside the bed. "You don't like men or prick. What's the angle?"

Her face turned pale, her blue eyes flared. "Oh, you smart-ass! Get the hell out of here!"

"Right," he grinned. "Then you can call your girlfriend and finish."

"You egotistical sonofabitch!" she snapped. She slid from the bed on the opposite side. She stood there uncertainly, breathing hard.

He turned, his cock shrinking, and walked out into the living room. He began to pick up his clothes and put them on. Just as he finished, he heard the bedroom door open again. She stood there in a robe, her face still drained of color.

"Thanks for the tip about this Daniels girl," he said, zipping up his fly. "If you ever decide you want a prick and a good screw, let me know."

She sneered. "You make me sick!"

"It was a good try, beautiful," he grinned. He walked to the door and opened it. He shot her a wink, went out, and banged the panel shut.

He made a mental note to visit the Oscar Stern Insurance Company office on Monday and get a good look at Jessica Daniels. He liked the name Jessica. Different. And screw Alexa he hoped he'd never see her again.

CHAPTER FOUR

Jessica looked up from her typewriter and saw the tall, big man talking to Chanelle, the pretty receptionist at Oscar Stern Insurance, and something happened. She felt a hot, sweet twinge between her legs.

Jessica had had a boring weekend. Amy had tried to talk her into going with John Castle and a blind date on Sunday up to a lakeshore resort north of the city, but she had refused. Amy meant well, but blind dates were out. Jessica had tried that before.

The guy Chanelle was flirting with wasn't exactly handsome, but he seemed so overpoweringly virile and appealing that Jessica couldn't take her eyes off him. It was Monday morning. Oscar Stern hadn't appeared yet, and it was Jessica's duty as his private secretary to handle knotty problems in his absence. She was very good at it, too. When Stern was out of town, Jessica was in charge.

The guy, who was at least six feet three or maybe more, glanced at Jessica. Chanelle turned, indicating to Jessica that he wanted to see her.

Heart pounding, Jessica reluctantly stood up and moved over beside the reception desk.

"Oh, Jessica," Chanelle gurgled. "This is Mister Randall Smith. He has a problem with a policy..."

Jessica trembled and almost lost her voice. Generally, she was very smooth with customers or prospective customers, but this guy was so disconcerting that she felt herself blushing. She was glad it didn't show on her dark skin.

"Would you like to step into Mr. Stern's office?" she found herself saying.

He smiled, and that bugged her even more. She wasn't looking down at him, for one thing. She led the way into the posh inner office, hoping desperately he liked the looks of her ass and legs. Chanelle giggled as the door closed.

"Mr. Stern should be in any moment," Jessica began, pointing to a chair in front of the big desk. "Could I help you, Mr. Smith?"

"I'm sure of it," he grinned, and again she felt a sweet thrill between her thighs. She was glad she was wearing one of her best frocks, with vertical black and white stripes that showed a lot of leg and delineated her thrusting tits. She stood beside the desk, and for once in her life, she didn't feel as tall as usual.

Damn! she thought dizzily; I believe he likes what he sees! Martha has told me so many times when I saw the right guy, my clit would get stiff, and that's just what it's doing. I wish I could flirt as easily as these other girls do, like Chanelle. Or Alexa. If he sees her, I'm dead.

He said he was thinking about changing policies on his car, as he wasn't satisfied with his present coverage. He told her he was from Los Angeles, in New York on business. She had time to notice that he wore no wedding ring. She said she was sure the Stern agency could give him just what he wanted.

A few moments later, she led him out of the office, getting his promise he would drop back later and see Stern. Just as he was walking by Chanelle's desk, Alexa came wiggling out of the office where she worked.

"Well, Jay," she gushed, posing with her tits pushed forward. "What a nice surprise!"

Jessica felt an instant surge of wild jealousy. It was crazy, too. She had just met him, and obviously, Alexa already knew him, the bitch!

"I took your suggestion, Alexa," he said a little coolly. He wasn't responding to her beauty; he acted as if she was just another secretary. Typist was the right word. He smiled at Jessica and moved toward the exit. "I'll see you later."

Jessica felt a cozy beating of her heart, a fine warmth spreading through her body. The expression on Alexa's pretty face was almost laughable. She had been snubbed. She shot Jessica a dirty look and twitched back to her desk at the rear. Chanelle, who had been watching the whole show, giggled at Jessica.

"He likes you. Wow! What a specimen."

Jessica didn't trust her voice. She winked at Chanelle and returned to her desk, still floaty. Her pussy was turning wet! The way she felt was simply incredible. "Love at first sight" was ridiculous. She had never believed in it, but that sweet glow in her crotch said more than her mind did.

She let her thoughts wander back to Alexa. It seemed a little odd that the curvy blonde was so attracted to him. She spent most of her time around girls, and she had been wanting to set something up with Jessica for a long time.

I may be hard up, Jessica thought, but I don't need pussy. She was really pissed off when I wouldn't move in with her.

Oh, she dates guys when she wants to go out, but if she gets her hooks into Jay, I'll murder her! Ohhh, damn. I never felt this way in my life.

A few moments later, as Jessica started to go to the can, Chanelle took a call on the switchboard, shot a glance at Jessica, and then rang her extension. Jessica picked up the receiver, her heart thudding.

"Hello, beautiful," came the voice she hoped for.

A tingly thrill shot along her thighs to her pussy. Her fingers trembled. "Is this Mister Smith?" she said quaveringly.

"Hell, call me Jay," he said warmly. "You know who it is. What about having lunch with me?"

"You're a pretty fast worker," she said, more at ease on the phone than she had been in front of him. Her clit said, yes, yes. Her nipples were even tingling and stiffening. She was tempted to make some catty remark about Alexa, but she didn't. He was calling her, not the flashy blonde.

"Well, yes," she said, finally.

"Good!" he answered, obviously pleased. "Shall I meet you out front around noon?"

"Sounds okay," she breathed, her heart leaping. She didn't want him to run into Alexa again. Evidently, he didn't want that to happen either.

"I like your dress, Jessica," he murmured. His voice had just the right tone of depth and sexiness.

She trembled like a schoolgirl. "Oh, you're just saying that."

He chuckled. "See you soon, and I'll tell you more, beautiful." The dial tone buzzed in her ear. She dropped the receiver, and Chanelle smiled. "I knew he'd cadi you."

"Oh, you little twitch," Jessica laughed.

A moment later, when she went to the can, she was on cloud nine.

He called me "beautiful", she thought, trembling. God! What a man he is. He's had lots of girls, though. I hope I can act mature and sophisticated. He's just the right age and everything. I hope he isn't married after all. Oh, hell, I can't let one little date throw me.

She examined her reflection in the bathroom mirror and felt a wash of her old shyness and inferiority. But her dark, large eyes had a bright sparkle, and her titties seemed to push her bodice out farther than usual. Her pussy was still damp, and her whole crotch tingled.

Under different circumstances, she would have been tempted to lock the door and play herself into an orgasm. The urgency was sharp and strong. Not now, though! She would just have to wait until she got home to the apartment. After all the excitement of watching Amy and John and listening while he had bounced her in bed, she hadn't had to relieve herself again.

I sure need it now, she thought, trembling. She remembered other times when she had eased her sexual appetites in this very bathroom, and a wave of shame passed through her being. If she could get a steady, maybe she wouldn't have to go that route anymore.

* * *

That long-legged slut, Alexa thought, watching Jessica return from her trip to the can. I'll bet she was in there playing with herself again. I know she does it. Shit! I threw them together, and he'll be in her panties in a day or two, maybe even sooner. I'll get even with that son-of-a-bitch somehow, and Jessica, too. I wanted that hot, tight pussy, and now he's going to get it. I'll mess them up, just wait and see!

She glanced out toward Chanelle, the pretty black receptionist. There was a choice young tidbit ready to be plucked. Chanelle was having trouble with her boyfriend, so she would be ready for a screw. She would be something to work on while Alexa decided what to do about Jessica and that bastard, Jay.

* * *

Jay sat in the shadows of the cafe and bar where he had taken Jessica to lunch and looked across the table at the beautiful, sexy brunette. Man, she had it, and a lot of it. Her black, glistening hair, cut rather close to her face, gave her model's profile an extra attractiveness. Her full, sensual mouth was perfection. The jaunty cones of her breasts, shaped cleverly by the frock, made his cockhead tingle and his mouth water.

She was so excited her hands trembled a little when they moved. She had a young-girl naiveness that was very refreshing after the almost universal brassiness of most gals her age, the "liberated" broads who had almost forgotten how to act like females. She was also very bright, and smart she knew the insurance business inside out, and Stern was no dummy letting her run the show when he was gone. What a beautiful, firm ass and fine long legs. He wasn't surprised to find out that she did part-time modeling.

And she was very definitely inhibited about her height. He didn't mind that one damn bit.

He discovered that she lived with her widowed mother and a younger sister; she was unattached and as shy and hesitant around him as a teenager from the country. This would take some very adroit handling. The thought of getting his hands on her made his nuts ache.

"Would you go out with me tonight, Jessica?" he asked.

She bit her lip. "Are you teasing me? Wouldn't you rather be seen with a pretty blonde like Alexa?"

"Look, I've seen too many like her," he smiled.

"Where would you like to go?" she asked, not meeting his gaze.

"What would you like? Dancing, a movie, or just driving around? You name it."

* * *

They were parked on a rise of ground, with the nose of his car facing a display of lights far beneath. It was around ten in the evening, a very glorious evening so far. They had stopped at a small tavern in Northtown and had a couple of beers and played pool. She had asked to drive around, and now, with the seat pushed way back to accommodate their long legs, Jessica knew he was going to start playing with her.

She sat under the steering wheel, with Jay at her right. They had just changed places. She had spent a solid hour showering and getting dressed for him. She had finally picked a short skirt and a blouse that swept low in front, her thinnest undies, and her most expensive perfume. She was still slightly dazed by the rapid turn of events.

Martha and Amy had kidded her unmercifully about her date, and when he had dropped by the apartment at eight, her mother and sister had seemed very impressed with him. Of course, Amy had poured on the charm. He had noticed her, all right. Most men did.

He scooted closer to Jessica and slid his left arm across her shoulders. She shivered, her panties already turning wet. Her clit had been tingling ever since she had climbed into his big, luxurious Dodge. Now, it was aching!

My first real date, she thought. I hope I don't blow it! He can't realize what he does to me.

"You haven't been around much, have you, Jessica?" he murmured in her ear. His arm tightened, and a sweet tremor ran the length of her body.

"No," she said, her voice quaky. "Who wants to date a mile-high girl?"

"Forget that," he murmured. His right hand slipped around her waist. "I like what I see, understand?"

A delicious warmth invaded her whole being, and she shivered again. It was all so new and wonderful, so furiously exciting, she could understand how some girls got hooked on their very first big date. Her man-hunger was so fierce she could hardly believe it. The ache in her crotch simply took possession of her.

But even if he did want to get to her, she was different. She was no junior high virgin burning for prick. She was twenty-one and on the pill. She didn't consider herself a virgin because she had used a dildo too often, and he wouldn't expect to find a maidenhead anyway. Cherries were old-fashioned in the sexy seventies. He would want a girl who knew how to screw.

His lips touched her cheek, and his right hand slipped up her waist to her breast-bulges. She shuddered, turning her head, her nipples stiff in her thin bikini bra, her clit as hard as the end of her little finger.

Jay's cock pushed up along his belly, the old familiar ache for pussy giving his knob a terrific bigness. She was all softness and willingness, shivering with excitement, breathing unevenly. Those beautiful long legs were slightly parted, and enough starlight came in the front seat to show her skirt hem back almost to her beautiful ass. The sweet, ripe fullness of her breasts lured his fingers.

He remembered when the door of the apartment had opened. When he had seen her all dressed up for her date, as excited as a teenager, there had been a quick thrill in his groin. He remembered the size and luxury of the living room, her attractive and sexy younger sister, Amy, and her surprisingly young-looking mother, Martha. It was easy to see from whom the girls had inherited their charm and voluptuous appeal their very high-class mother.

Amy was some bundle, too. Nothing shy or bashful about her. She had been having fun with men for a long time; he could tell. She was just a little over average height, with sensational tits and a sexy ass and long legs. She had gushed and flirted with him, letting him know he could get in her panties if he ever took the initiative.

Well, Jessica said Amy had steadies, but eighteen-year-old

girls were always looking. Right now, he didn't want to think about Amy. Old sister was shivering and waiting for feels, and he sure as hell wasn't going to delay it.

He hadn't tried any swift stuff with Jessica. Sitting in the tavern with her, playing pool in the nearly deserted lounge, he had let things develop naturally. People had stared when he had walked in with her. She was a startlingly attractive girl. Her tallness, the exquisite curvature of her ass and breasts, had drawn a wolf whistle from an old codger at the bar. The comely barmaid had mentioned that she had once seen Jessica modeling downtown. It had been a very pleasant half hour.

As he brushed his lips onto her full, sensual mouth and fit his palm on the sweet firmness of a thinly covered breast, a little moan rose in her throat. Her lips opened, both of her arms slid around his neck, and her long right thigh pressed against his left leg. She shuddered.

Terrific!

He believed the expert who said that girls knew how to kiss without instruction. He had bussed his share of eager chicks and hadn't found one yet who didn't appreciate long, careful tongue-and-mouth contact. The older ones liked it, too. Maybe it made them feel young again.

The cling and hungriness of Jessica's mouth swelled his cockhead. Her arms tightened, and she shuddered again. He began to stroke with his tongue. She moaned, and her long thighs began to open. The poor girl was totally famished with male attention. Her lips quivered, and her tongue started to flick against his. Beautiful!

The firmed, coned perfection of her breast, the feel of her

nipple inside the lightweight covering, charged his passion. Man, what a pair! Only her height had kept her from enjoying what other girls of her age and sexual inclinations had been tasting for years, and now that she was starting, she was like a jungle tigress. Her supple strength was startling, humbling.

He started to open her blouse.

* * *

Jessica heard herself whine with need, and she couldn't help it. His mouth, his sliding tongue, his overpowering maleness, and the possessive press of his fingers on her swollen, aching breast started the wrenchingly sweet thrills in her crotch. She was shivering toward a climax! She had denied herself all day, ever since he had walked into the office, and now the long-delayed ache was bunching in her crotch, tensing her clitoris and hardening her nipples.

Oh, I hope he doesn't think I'm some kind of nympho! she thought wildly. God! Here it comes! I can't hold it any longer! My first sexy kiss, my first tittie feel, and I'm getting my goodies! Ohhh, Oh, Ohh!

The burning twinges of her exploding passion shook her whole body. The honeyed pulling along her thighs, the aching slowness of her rise to peak out, and the hard pulsing of her clitoris broke her mouth from his. She moaned fiercely, her thighs shook, her ass wiggled. For heavenly, pounding heartbeats, she was wild! Nothing like this had ever happened before! It was tearing through her loins, surging in hot waves along her legs and out to the point of her clitoris!

"Ohh, Ohh!" she cried, clutching him with all her strength. "Ohhh, Gog!"

As she finally softened, feeling the exquisite pangs of relief in her crotch and breasts, she panted against his throat.

"Ohhhh, Jay!"

"You sweet thing, you," he murmured, cuddling her tittie in his big strong hand. What would happen when he stroked her bare flesh? She was afraid to consider! She would flip clear out.

Something Amy had said flamed across her thoughts. "Don't get too heavy with it, honey. Make it a fun thing, or you'll scare him off, sure as hell. Sure, you gotta get involved to make it good, but you start coming on too strong, and he'll fly the coop."

Good advice, if only she could manage it. "Mmmmm, some fun for me," she breathed. "What about you, honey?"

What I'd like to say is I'm completely nuts about you. I want to marry you and have that big thing in me all the time. But hell! I'm just a date, a big, tall freak he probably feels sorry for.

He was silent for a few seconds, and then he chuckled. "Look, don't worry about that, Jessica. I want you to have fun, understand?"

"Ohhhh, wow!" she giggled. "Am I ever!"

She settled in cozily against him, her left arm dropping across his lap, her right arm still around his neck. She was half-turned above the waist so he could play with her breasts. The delicious twinges of aftermath made her dizzy. Her pussy was all swollen and leaky. Her tits ached for touches, her mouth ached for more tongue.

"Would you consider going to my motel, Jessica?" he murmured, his right hand lifting to her blouse.

She trembled, her clit stiffening again. "Honey, I thought you'd never ask!" she exclaimed. Be casual and lighthearted about it. Be like Amy said she was. That had been true with John Castle she had watched the whole thing. Don't get heavy! She wanted more dates with Jay, lots more! Nowadays, a piece of ass was just a piece of ass.

If I'm not good for him, he can sure find other chicks, she thought. Amy would like to make it with him. He noticed her wiggling around, too. Oh, hell! Even if he never dates me again, I'll have one night to remember.

When he released her and moved out of the car, walking around the front to return to his place behind the wheel, she was glad they would soon be in a place where she could use the facilities. Her panties were a mess.

As the dome light went on the second time, she saw his eyes glide between her long, dark thighs. Her panties, lacy pink, were visible, and she didn't try to draw her miniskirt forward. He smiled, and the light went out. She snuggled up against him, keeping her legs open naturally!

* * *

Jay wasn't too surprised about Jessica's reactions. She was very naive and trying not to show it. After all, she was around twenty-one, an age when most beautiful girls were either married or had been pronged plenty of times. Her violent orgasm, after a little hugging and tongue-kissing, told him just how hungry and hot she was. She was trying to be very sophisticated about the whole scene, but he knew better.

Well, every girl had to justify her actions somehow. She was a delicious chick those long legs and fine thrusting tits were sensational. Her mouth was just as eager as he had expected it to be. His cock was still rock-hard and oozing slickness, his nuts ached for a blast, but of course, he would give her one hell of a good time before he slipped it to her.

He drove away from the turnout and headed downtown, letting his right hand drop down between her thighs. She trembled and breathed warmly on his neck, her left leg pressing in close. The feel of her thigh, sleekly nyloned, made his fingers tremble. Sonofabitch! What a lot of girl, what beautiful assets.

Jessica moved ahead of him into the luxurious motel suite, and her legs shook. Having his hand between them on the drive into the city's center had brought a new surge of wetness in her pussy. He couldn't realize what a caress like that, altogether new in her experience, did to her nerves! She was feverish for another climax. Her clit felt an inch long!

She heard him lock the door and put the chain on. She clutched her handbag and ran to the bathroom, her heart pounding so wildly she was afraid to speak. Inside the brightly tiled and decorated can, she leaned against the door and hugged herself.

He wants more of me! she thought sweetly. He wants to screw me, and I'm dying for it. That lump in his pants is so big I wonder if I can take all of it! Ohhh, damn. I'm finally going to get fucked! I'll have something to tell Amy. She won't be the only girl in the family to know what a cock feels like!

When she raised her skirt and lowered her panties to dab away the excess juices, she could hardly believe how swollen her pussy was. Her labia had always been outcurved, like her mouth, but now they were puffed way out. Her clit was so tender she knew she didn't dare touch it a certain way. She wanted to have her next climax with him, and the next and the next...

* * *

Jay took a chair and had a smoke, his finger shaky. His cock wouldn't go down it was too eager for hot, new pussy. But he had to take it real easy and slow. He doubted she had ever been screwed, and the prospect of giving her her first hot prick made him shiver.

A little preparation might make things better for her. He cut the overhead light and turned on a small lamp beside the king-size bed. He took off his jacket and dug out the bottle of good bourbon he had bought that afternoon. He had ordered ice earlier. It was in a metal container. He uncovered two fresh glasses the maid had brought in. He ladled out ice and mixed two highballs. He had already learned that she liked booze and water when she had hard liquor. A very practical kind of girl no nonsense.

She came out of the bathroom at last, wide-eyed, obviously pleased about the dim interior of the room. He grinned and held out her drink.

"Mmmmm, you're spoiling me," she giggled nervously.

He steered her to a small sofa and sat down at her right. She wiggled in close, her uneven, excited breathing stirring his glands again. A wave of perfume and girl aroma, delightfully mingled, teased his senses.

"You know what got me about you, Jessica?" he grinned.

"Nooo..."

"When you leaned over the pool table to make that bank shot, I got a good look at your ass and those nice long legs."

"Oh, you devil," she breathed. "What about when we were parked?"

"Sensational," he chuckled. "Do you know you have a very sexy walk?"

"Mmm! I'm glad you think so."

She was losing her first nervousness. Good. "Would you like some music, Jessica?"

"Yes, I'd love it," she said, taking a sip of her highballs. The way her lips touched the rim of the glass, teasing it with sensual intimacy, tingled the head of his cock. He moved to the radio and found a music station. When he had the volume right, he returned to the sofa. She was much more relaxed now. He slid his left arm across her shoulders and eyed the fine sweet cones of her tits in the thin, revealing blouse. She trembled, her head turned for a kiss.

CHAPTER FIVE

Alexa Daniels drove slowly by the motel Jay Romero called home while he was in New York and pulled her car in near a sidewalk phone booth. She had learned where he was staying on her date with him. Earlier, she had been parked across the street, and when he had driven up with Jessica, Alexa had waited a while, her heart pounding with excitement.

Now for the dirty blow. She moved into the phone booth, dropped in a dime, and dialed.

* * *

Jessica felt Jay's tongue slide voluptuously into her hungry mouth and felt his right hand on her blouse, where a few buttons would open the door to her tingling breasts. She appreciated the little delay while he had served her a drink. She was now perfectly at ease. The preliminaries had been utterly delightful, and now it was time for the real thing, the nitty-gritty.

The sweet, hot ache in her crotch made her shudder. His tongue moved in and out, in and out, sending zingy thrills to her tits and clitpoint. It was cozy and wild, almost like in the front seat of his car, only this time, he was going much farther – all the way!

His fingers opened the top of her blouse, then moved down to the next button. She moaned and coiled her arms around his neck, opening her lips wide. Everything was lovely! They were alone, music was playing softly, the liquor flamed in her veins, and her whole body was alive to him. The slide of his virile tongue bunched more thrills in her pelvis. Her titties were swelling and straining to get out of her bra, and her pussy leaked more juice into her panties.

The front of her blouse was wide open now. His fingers shaped a tittie, and the thin pink unpadded bra didn't seem to exist. Her nipple erected in its nylon cup as his tongue stroked deeper into her mouth. She remembered Amy's boldness with John Castle, but she couldn't be that aggressive yet.

God! I love it! She thought dizzily. Every little touch and feel! I never felt so turned on all over! My temperature must be a hundred and ten! When I play with myself, it's all centered in my crotch. I like to hold my titties in my left hand and feel them swell but this is all so much better! Ohh, I'm dying for another cum!

Still nibbling at her puffy lips, he caught her left hand and drew it down to his basket.

Hesitantly but eagerly, she pressed her fingers on his big cock-lump. Her thighs began to spread, and she urged her right thigh against his leg. The feel of his manhood, even covered, surged her achy need higher. What a man! His cock was huge!

His hand returned to her breasts. He found the front opener on her bra, a tricky little thing Amy had suggested, and just as his fingers closed around her tender, expanded breast, just as she felt her stiffened nipple caress his palm, the sweet tingles of delight started tensing her clitoris.

"Ohh!" she cried, her hips curving upward. "Oh, Ohh God!"

I'm cumming for him again! she thought crazily. Oh, sweet Jesus! It was never like this, or this, or this! The sweetness is ripping the hell out of my crotch! I'm cumming harder than I ever did! He told me he wanted me to have lots of fun, and it's so much fun I'm going to scream!

* * *

Jay heard Jessica's fierce whine of delight, felt the delicious arch of her breast in his hand, the quick lift of her ass, and his prick almost burst out of his shorts and pants. The involuntary jerks of her long, sexy thighs, her total involvement with her climax, expanded his ego. Man, she went off like a cannon! The first one in the front seat had been a ringer, but she was getting much more from number two.

The way she hunched and wiggled her ass when she blew was something a man dreamed about. Sonofabitch. He hadn't even played with her pussy. The poor girl had been neglected for too many years, and she was trying to make up for lost time. And he had been lucky enough to find her, all six feet of her. Fantastic!

She softened in the curve of his left arm, her eyes closed, her fleshy lips parted, her uneven breathing much sweeter than the music from the radio. Her shivers of aftermath communicated from her breast to his hand. He looked down at the fine, sweet taper of her long thighs and the curve of her cunny in the fancy pink panties where a vertical patch of wetness showed over her crevice. Beautiful!

"Ohh, you big devil, you," she breathed, opening her eyes and staring up at him with such intensity he was humbled. Her left hand still rested on his prick-tent. She looked down at it and shivered again. Her fingers began to play gently. Her exquisite thighs spread farther.

"Let's get some clothes off, Jessica," he whispered.

"Ohhh, yes!" she breathed, shuddering. "Yes!"

* * *

Jessica almost hated to move. She was so deliciously weak and shivery, so blissfully relaxed after her orgasm; she was in a sweet daze. He liked her high, jutting tits and her long tawny thighs, liked her ass and her mouth. He didn't care how tall she was!

She suddenly remembered a thing her mother had said rather jokingly. "Honey, don't worry about being tall. My daddy used to say a long board made the best teeter."

God, I hope I'm the best screwing he ever had! she thought. I'll do anything to keep him coming back for more, anything! I'll suck him and let him eat me; I'll screw on top or sideways or any way. Sweet Jesus! I've dreamed so much about what I'd do for a big, handsome lover I don't know where to start!

* * *

Jay started to move from the sofa, and a sound outside interrupted his concentration. A squeal of tires on macadam, car doors slamming. Some punk giving the tire manufacturers a break. He would have to get a motel farther out of the city's center. He had picked this one because it wasn't far from Melanie Welch's big home.

He had an appointment to see her the next afternoon. Judging from the way she had sounded on the phone, he was afraid she wanted his prick as much as she wanted advice on how to handle her insurance claim. Oh, well, she was a bit on the plump side, but she had a beautiful pair of tits and a good ass. A frustrated thirty-year-old swinger, beyond a doubt.

Now that she had pushed her aging husband down some steps and broken his neck and was ready to collect his insurance, she was also ready to start enjoying herself. Somehow, he had to prove she was a murderess.

Suddenly, he heard rapid footsteps and a loud banging on his motel door. Jessica jumped like he'd stuck a pin in her pretty ass, her fine glow fading. He cursed, waved her toward the bathroom, and walked to the door.

"Police!" came snarlingly from beyond the panel. "Open up!"

The sonsofbitches! What the hell was going on? Some damned mistake, beyond a doubt. He held his temper, being familiar with police routine, and took the chain off, unlocking the door. He threw it open and saw a uniformed officer and a pale-faced plainclothesman.

"You better have a warrant," he snapped.

The plainclothesman's mouth formed an obscenity, and they came busting inside. They began a quick search.

"Somebody's going to pay for this," Jay said coldly. "What the hell are you looking for?"

"We got a tip you and some broad are having a pill party," the plainclothesman growled.

"Shit," Jay growled. "Look around, Dad. You got the wrong grapevine."

Ten minutes later, they were gone, and a very frightened Jessica sat uneasily beside him, her hands shaking. The rotten cocksuckers had scared her silly. They had insisted on searching the bathroom; they had seen Jessica and made a note of it. Jay had the officers' names, and in the morning, he would have an attorney. Narcs had been making illegal break-ins all over the country, and the government was being sued for millions. Somebody sure as hell was going to pay for this break-in, too.

"I... I'd better go home," Jessica quavered, not looking at him. "This is awful..."

He swore again. She was right, of course. The whole scene was bad; the whole thing with her might be blown to hell.

* * *

When Jessica reached the Daniels home, she was glad her mother and sister were already in bed. She rushed into her bedroom, closed the door, and fell into a chair, tears of frustration wetting her eyes.

Her beautiful evening was ruined! The horrible shock of the interruption, the knowing leers on the faces of the two policemen when they had opened the bathroom door, still made her sick inside.

Ohhhh, damn them! she thought. Any anonymous tip, they said. I think I know who made that phone call, that rotten bitch of Alexa! But I can probably never prove it. Jay suspects her, too. Oh, I wanted to stay in the motel with him, but I was cold as ice inside! He knew it. God! I may never see him again!

I was all ready to go crazy with him, my whole body ached for him, and it still does, but my pussy feels clammy! Caught in a shack job. And I didn't even get to see his prick, let alone have it in me!

Gradually, the terror began to leak away. Jay had said he would call her in the morning. He was going to sue the city, so he would be involved with an attorney and a lot of other things, and it might be days before they could have a relaxed, cozy date.

After a shower, after she had put on a thin nightie and prepared for bed, she began to feel better. The whole evening had been dreamy until the awful interruption. She was sure he did want to see her again. She had climaxed violently two delicious times in his embrace, so the night hadn't been a total loss! She had a big, virile boyfriend.

A light tap on the connecting bathroom door told her Amy was awake and wanted to talk. Well, for once, she had something exciting to tell her sexy sister!

"You're home kind of early, honey," Amy said, wiggling over to the bed and perching on the rim. Her red nightie didn't hide much. "I heard you taking a shower. I hope you were washing out what I think you were!"

"Oh, don't be so filthy," Jessica objected.

"You look pretty pleased with yourself," Amy giggled. "He's some stud. How was it, anyway?"

Jessica trembled. A little exaggeration wouldn't hurt a

thing. She knew Amy blew things out of shape she liked to brag about her conquests.

"Oh, he got me real good," Jessica smiled. She rolled her eyes. "Like, wow!"

"Nnnnn!" Amy giggled. "See what you've been missing?"

Jessica felt her passion start to rise again. Thinking about her orgasms was stiffening her clitoris. Not getting his prick, after all the sweet preliminaries, had been just terrible!

"Does he really know how to work a girl over?" Amy asked slyly.

"You know it, honey," Jessica smiled, feeling rather smug. Her pussy was turning wet again, her nipples stiffening against the hug of her nightie.

She knew she would have to play with herself before she could sleep.

Amy sighed and wiggled toward the connecting door. "Well, don't get too heavy with it, honey. You could get hurt. But I am glad you're finding out what a prick feels like!"

"Oh, get your ass out of here," Jessica laughed. "There's nothing like it, absolutely nothing!"

"That's what mother always told us," Amy said, winking. She twitched out of sight and closed the door.

Jessica trembled, lifting her hands to her swelling titties. She closed her eyes and imagined Jay was playing with her nipples again. The hot urgency fanned out from her crotch. She went to her vanity, opened the lower drawer, and drew out her trusty dildo. She crawled into bed and flicked out the bedside lamp. In the cozy darkness, she stretched and let her thoughts wander back over the wonderful evening right up to the start of the jarring interruption.

She had a boyfriend! She had been adored, admired, kissed, and played with, and he was going to take her out again. It made everything so different and made life worth living. Her fantasy had sharp reality because she had been there! Not all the way, but that would be next time.

I should wait for our next date, but I can't! she thought, pressing the dildo between her thighs. Those awful cops scared me silly. I'm okay now, and I have to cum! I'll imagine he has that big cock snuggled in my pussy, then it will start in and out. Ohhhh, damn! I need him so much right now!

She didn't feel as guilty about masturbating as she had at one time when she was younger. She had inherited a deep sensuality from her mother, and nowadays, chicks everywhere were doing what men did when they couldn't find a woman.

She was sure when it came down to the real nitty-gritty in bed, she could give Jay a good screw. She had read the right books and looked at diagrams of various positions. Her big fear was that she would want to screw too much! Her two delicious orgasms with him had just touched her raging need.

But he seemed to understand this. A cum was a cum she didn't care what he did with her body to send her whirling into spasms of sexual delight. The more fun she had, the better he liked it. Ohhh, he was some man her real dream lover!

With her left hand, she eased her tingling breasts out of the top of her nightie and spread her thighs far apart. She touched the head of the dildo against her moistened labia, teased her nipples into achy stiffness, and slowly pushed the artificial prick into her cunny.

She moaned and arched her back. Ohhh, the thing had never felt so delicious! In her dream, he was above her, between her long legs, and it was his prick sliding hotly to her depths, sounding her need. She remembered what Martha had told her about pleasing a man, and she tightened her vaginal muscles. She had practiced it many times, but she wanted to have it down pat. For the past year or so, she'd felt she was becoming very proficient.

Tonight, her membranes were responding in a new, delicious way because the right guy had almost made it in her. Ohhhh, yes!

She recalled her first serious talk about sex with her mother at the age of fifteen. She had been playing with her pussy for relief for years before that, of course. It had embarrassed her to learn that Martha was fully aware of her sneaky little habit, but after a long conversation, she felt much better.

"Honey," Martha had said, "you know why so many of these chicks have trouble with their men? They don't give them a good fuck! Just having a pussy isn't enough, Jessica. Every chick has one. It's what you do with it that keeps a guy hanging around and coming home on time."

After that, she had used her long middle finger in her pussy. Getting some inner action had taken several months. She had enjoyed herself with her clitoris for so long that she felt kind of dead inside. But gradually, she was able to clench her vagina, and it made her cums better and harder!

"A pussy needs exercise like any other part of the body,

honey," Martha had laughed. "Having your enjoyment is good for you; it makes you feel more like you're alive. You have to kind of understand how a man thinks about sex. They like a gal that's hot. It's ninety percent physical with them, see."

Jessica adored Martha for giving out all that intimate advice, and of course, Amy had gotten the benefits of that sex instruction, too. The only thing was Amy had been screwing for years, and beyond a doubt, she was a very hot piece. And she liked Jay...

Shuddering, Jessica held the dildo firmly by the handle and practiced coming up on it. Ohhh, it was good! Hump, hump, hump. Tighten the pussy. Mmmmmm! Rest. Drag out the fun. She wouldn't need to flick the switch on the handle tonight. The battery-powered dildo vibrated almost too swiftly when it was turned on, but it was great for a panting quickie.

Oh, I hope he lets me screw on top, Jessica thought, feeling the sweet thrills chase along her body. Amy sure goes for it. And the man can last longer that way, too. Oh, Jesus, I can hardly wait! This is going to be a boomer!

She hunched again, letting the shaft slide wetly against her achy clit. Ohhhh! Not too much of that! She could bring the cum very swiftly by tickling her little "boy in the boat," but she wanted to dream some more, wanted to play with her need, and have a wild, big orgasm.

She remembered Jay's compliments about her legs and ass. He liked the way she walked, her hot mouth, her pointy firm titties. They were really sticking up high tonight. Her nipples were super-sensitive, stiff, and tingly. She remembered the feel of his hand on her breasts, the slow, excruciating sweep to her front-seat climax. She wanted his tongue in her throat again. Ohh, yes!

* * *

Amy stood in the darkness of the bathroom, her ear to the door to Jessica's bedroom. Jessica was doing what Amy expected, having some fun before she went to sleep. The faint, rhythmic sighing of the bed, three or four creaks followed by a rest, told the story.

It seemed kind of strange after a date with a guy as sexy as Jay. Jessica had come home rather early. Maybe he didn't like her after all.

I'd sure like to get my hands on him, Amy thought, shivering. He sure looked me over. I'll find out where he's staying and call him. What Jessica doesn't know won't hurt her.

Amy hadn't played with herself for a week or more. The weekend with John Castle had been a blast. At the lake, he had rented a nice cabin. They had gone swimming and boating. They had danced at a little resort spot in the evening, and after returning to the cabin, they had fucked half the night. Delicious!

But Sunday morning had been the best. Drinks the night before always made her extra hot. She had climaxed ten times before noon, and he had poured two more shots of jism into her twitchy cunt. He was pretty good with his seven inches, but she had an idea that Jay would be better. He had the look of a real gashhound.

John didn't go much for oral sex. Amy was sure Jay would

go the route. He had that certain hunger in his eyes. Well, something had happened between Jessica and Jay, or poor Jessica wouldn't be humping and panting in her bedroom all alone, probably using her artificial prick again.

Amy had tried the dildo a few times while Jessica was at work. It was okay; Amy could come with it, but the real thing was so much better! Martha had an imitation cock too. It was larger and longer than Jessica's, it had more of a knob on the end, and the vibrating mechanism had three speeds! When she had kidded her mother about it, Martha had laughed.

"I hardly ever shift into high gear, honey. That low speed makes me cum nice and slow..."

They had both giggled. Martha was such a sophisticated, mature woman. Not bad looking either, for forty-two. She managed to have a steady most of the time, and right now, she was screwing Oscar Stern, too. Martha claimed the married ones his age were really better than single men. Obviously, Martha was a good fuck. All that experience behind her...

"Ohhhh!" came dramatically from Jessica's bedroom. The mattress sighed faster. She was starting her short, fast strokes!

Amy shivered, dropping her right hand down to her crotch. Hearing her sister huff and puff to a climax did beautiful things for her own clit. She teased the rising nub of flesh, arching her hips forward. Ohhh, yes! She didn't feel guilty about playing with her pussy any more than Jessica did. Martha had explained everything to them; steady sex was a joy that every healthy woman needed. It was simply a lot more fun doing it with a guy.

Quietly, she left the bedroom, closed her own door, and

sank down on her bed. A reading lamp still glowed beside the bed. She left it on and sprawled her thighs apart. She placed both pillows under her head, squirmed her ass into a comfortable position, and returned her right hand to her cunny.

She liked to watch herself when she did her finger thing. Eager juice was forming between her pussy lips. She slicked her little nub of flesh and began to draw the thrills from her loins. John would be wanting a date soon, probably on Wednesday night, but that was a long time away.

It would be more pleasurable to think about Jay while she did it. Nnnnn! Right on! He was a hell of a man. Maybe he would like a younger girl than Jessica.

He's gonna get a chance at me, she thought, feeling her clit harden. The knifing thrills along her thighs were extra sweet. Her nipples stiffened delectably. Sometimes she didn't feel her titties when she was building her pleasure, but she decided to this time. With her free left hand, she eased her beautiful breasts from the clinging red nightie. John was pretty good with them, but she had an idea that Jay would be better.

Ohhhhh, yes! With her first finger on one side of her clit and her second finger on the other, she looked down at her sexy little girl-prick and watched the wet pink point begin to rise even higher. When she was ready to cum it was a quarter-inch thick and just as prominent. The covered length that didn't show was sensitive, too.

Ohhhh, almost! She shuddered and waited, prolonging the fun. The wrenching little zings of delight chased clear up to her swelling tits. It was going to be a good one. This was almost the best part, delaying the voluptuous sensations, dragging it out, as Martha had explained.

Her mother had told her to practice clenching her vagina, too, but she didn't quite go along with that. She could do that when she was screwing.

Carefully, she inched more thrills from her heated crotch. Love that clit! It was all ready to explode. Somehow, the thought of Jessica getting her thrills with Jay made Amy's passion stronger. She realized she would like to watch Jessica getting the cock, just as Jessica had watched her doing her thing. It was kind of dirty, but it would be really fun.

She wondered whether Jay had ever taken two girls to bed. Probably! A lot of hot young chicks were going that route, doubling up with some well-hung stud. It was kind of Lesbian, but it was supposed to be really wild. As long as she and Jessica didn't touch each other...

She almost squealed as the sweet pounding of her orgasm ripped her crotch. Mmmm! Ohhh, good!

CHAPTER SIX

Jay Romero punched the doorbell button beside the big front door of Melanie Welch's house on Pinewood Avenue, New York's most exclusive area of older homes. It was Tuesday afternoon. While he had called her the previous day, she had sounded very receptive. Knowing she'd never seen him up close at the car wash, he'd told her he was a representative of her insurance company, which was the truth, up to a point. He hadn't told her he was an investigator trying to keep her from cashing in a hundred grand, which was a lot of bread.

He'd had a busy morning. He had talked to one of the sharpest attorneys in New York, who had said he had a good chance of collecting from the city for a search of his quarters without a warrant. The sonsofbitches were going to pay plenty.

He had called Jessica, and her gratitude had been so sincere, her voice so sexy, he had got half a hardon just standing in the phone booth. She was over her fright. When he had suggested dropping by around eight, she had been as happy as a child. This time, he was going to score well. She knew it, and he knew it.

The door opened, and a surprisingly pretty Polynesian girl wearing a maid's uniform gave him a wide, interested smile and said Mrs. Welch was expecting him. The maid wiggled ahead of him and opened another door. Melanie lived in style. The maid giggled, and then he entered a big, plush living room. It was filled with French Provincial furniture, even a big grand piano. His first glimpses of Melanie had been downtown now he was seeing her in her own nest, and it was really something.

She came out of a chair, smiling warmly. She wore a kind of bright yellow and black hostess thing with wide slits down the sides that revealed glimpses of plump nyloned thigh and leg. Her brown hair was attractively waved, and her sensual mouth painted a bright carmine, a thing the mod broads were doing this season.

His file on her said she had been in show business in her earlier years, singing with a band. Her late husband had spotted her at a joint in Reno, and they had been married a few months later. No children. There was also a report that she had once been a high-priced whore in Las Vegas, working as a call-girl.

In one way, the living room did look like a fancy crib. It was all too posh and overdone. It was easy to see that she liked sex. She had a fine pair of tits, an observation he had made earlier, and a good rounded ass and very fine legs. The few wrinkles on her neck didn't really detract from her startling sensuality. She was thirty, and the odds were that she was a good piece of ass.

And her warm brown eyes said she wanted him to give her a try.

"So glad you called, Jay," she cooed, twitching up close. The first-name thing was apparently a show-business affectation. "Like a drink?"

"Maybe later," he smiled, watching the delicate sway of her tits against the shimmery covering of her expensive outfit. It was belted at the waist, giving her breasts a more provocative accent. The nipples poked at the cloth, and he suspected her breasts were supported only from underneath.

"Well, sit down, honey," she smiled, ass-swaying over to a plush wide sofa. A blast of expensive perfume teased his senses.

He followed, easing down to her right, where she had patted the fat cushion. She sighed deeply and gave him a drippy, meaningful stare.

"Are things about finished on the insurance policy?"

"Sure, a few little details to take care of," he grinned. "I'll have the local agent bring papers by for you to sign in a day or two. You understand this is quite a large amount of money..."

"Oh, I know. Frederick was so thoughtful." She looked sad for a moment, as if in mourning, then gave him a bright smile. "I'm going to sell the house and move to Boston. More things are going on there. You know, excitement."

"Sure," he said. "An attractive girl like you shouldn't be alone."

She giggled. Her eyes flicked at his basket and returned to his face. "Flatterer!"

"I think I will take that drink," he said. A well-stocked bar setup was in one corner of the big room.

"Good!" she bubbled. "I'll bet you're a scotch on the rocks kind of man."

"Right," he said. She wasn't moving, and he wasn't either. She leaned nearer. Her tongue wet her bright red lips, and she wiggled it invitingly. His cockhead tingled. He slid his left arm across the back of the sofa.

"I've been horribly lonesome, Jay," she whispered, her

silky right thigh grazing his left leg. "The funeral, that awful inquest..."

"Sure, I understand," he grinned. Easy as picking ripe fruit. She was ready; her voice on the phone had said so, and now her ripe body and hungry eyes were saying it again, only louder.

"Give me a kiss, and then I'll fix us a drink, huh?" she breathed.

I shouldn't try this when I'm taking Jessica out tonight, he thought. But I'm sure I can do more investigating in bed. I'd be a fool to pass it up, even if I never learn a damned thing.

A very slight movement of his left arm on her shoulders swayed her toward him. Her carmine lips opened, her tongue wiggling and waiting between them. She shivered.

He tightened his left arm and raised his right hand to her pert breasts so cleverly accented in the shimmery covering. He claimed her mouth just as his fingers claimed a tit. She shivered again, her mouth opening, her tongue snaking out. He had been right about her breasts. They were just under-cupped, the nipples and upper slopes pushed far out. He squeezed and felt the clamp of her mouth on his.

She moaned, writhing her lips against his, urging her tit more firmly into his palm. Her right thigh pushed silkily into his left leg. He held his tongue out of the way and let her use hers. It stabbed deeply, then began to coil and flirt. Her legs began to spread. She moaned again, her right arm winding around his neck, her left hand snaking to his basket.

When he happened to run into someone like Melanie, a quick, easy lay, he liked to be very clinical about it. Driving a hungry woman frantic was one of his favorite things. He realized that, in some ways, he would make a good male whore, a love machine, as one middle-aged woman had described him. Getting emotionally involved with a money-conscious broad like Melanie could be very dangerous, as her late husband had discovered.

It was just possible she hadn't had a good piece of ass for a while, but he doubted that. A really sensual woman always managed to get her screwing. For her, cock was a necessity; the signs stuck out all over her. Good. A fine, naive girl like Jessica was entirely different. He could become involved with her very easily. In fact, he already was.

After the shitty interruption the night before, he hadn't jacked off, after all. Giving a sexy girl her pleasure tempered his need. He could wait a long time for his enjoyment. After all, a turned-on chick could climax time after time with the right coaxing and playing. That was the secret of enjoying sex for any man past the age of twenty.

When he had been sixteen, with a perpetual hardon, a neighbor woman as old as his mother had coached him in the fine arts of screwing and playing. Her lessons he had never forgotten. She had taught him control. It had paid off during college, and even his wife had enjoyed his expertise in bed. But he was well rid of her thinking about her was a waste of time.

There was so much willing stuff running around, so many pill-liberated chicks dying for cock; it was a shame to miss all of them. Jessica's beautiful young sister was available, too. But he was afraid that if he banged her, he might lose Jessica. There was a very special girl.

Melanie's pressing fingers drew him back to the exciting present. She stroked her tongue in another flurry and shuddered. She breathed into his mouth.

"Damn! I don't need a drink, honey. Let's go in the bedroom, huh?"

"Sure," he grinned. "We can have a drink at intermission."

She giggled. She pressed his cock-lump. "That feels like a winner."

A talker. Well, some were, and some weren't. He liked it either way. He cuddled her other thinly sheathed breast, teasing the prominent nipple. She wiggled her shoulders, watching his hand, her breathing uneven. All systems said go.

She stood up, catching his playing hand. He got to his feet and followed her toward a hallway.

The room they entered was even more luxurious than the living area. The bed was huge, covered with brightly-hued pillows. There were love seats and mirrors. A thick red carpet covered the floor. There was even a big mirror on the ceiling, over the bed. He glanced up at it and chuckled.

"Frederick loved that," she laughed. She ran the zipper down her bodice and opened it, letting her tits out. She was proud of them, and with good reason. The clever underpadding didn't seem really necessary. Her breasts had a fine jut. The brown nipples were widely banded, pointing at him. They were already tumid and swollen.

"Not bad, huh?" she giggled, arching her tits forward.

He pursed his lips, and she giggled again. Slowly, she began to take her garment from her body, her dark eyes fastened on his basket. It was warm outside, so he wore no jacket. He unhitched his belt and removed his sports shirt.

Melanie shivered, her pussy tingling. It was already wet, her clit stiff with anticipation. What a beautiful specimen of virile manhood! Wide shoulders narrow hips, and quite handsome. He had a tremendous cock.

Frederick's sudden death had scared her steady. She had told him to stop hanging around and calling until her late husband's estate was settled. He wasn't really a very good screw, anyway. She was going to dump him and go south just as soon as possible.

New York was a square burg, and she had had a lot of trouble sneaking around on Frederick. He had been able to get a hardon only about twice a month however, she had given him a good screw when he was able. That was why an old man married a younger broad.

Although she didn't have the figure she had possessed in her call-girl days, she enjoyed sex more. Another thing she had missed while married to Frederick was an occasional girl fuck. Her new maid, an Americanized Polynesian, was developing. Teasing Tracy and getting her cute pussy to cum was nice for fill-in sex, but of course, cock was the best.

She had learned to enjoy lesbian pleasure in Las Vegas when she had doubled up with another call girl on a heavy date with a bigshot from the corn belt. The guy had wanted to watch her screw the other gal, and surprisingly, they had both reached a tremendous climax. The event had opened her eyes to a new dimension in sensual pleasures.

Frederick had been very square, of course. Now, she was

starting to swing. Even without the big insurance payoff, she would still be able to live high and indulge herself. She had it made. She suspected Jay was more than just an agent of the company he had the odor of fuzz but if he thought he was going to save his company any money, he was full of shit.

Tracy, the maid, had been out of the house when she had pushed Frederick down the stairs. No witnesses.

She stepped out of the hostess gown just as Jay kicked off his shoes and lowered his pants. His cock was ridged up so high the big knob almost cleared the band of his briefs. What a horse!

Anticipating that she would be undressing for him, she had put on a pair of very sheer red bikini panties, lace-trimmed in purple. Her nylons reached almost to her crotch. She still wore her heels. A glance in the mirror behind Jay said she looked her best. Men loved provocative undies, and obviously, he was no exception. Her crevice showed through the panties she'd had her pubic hair removed years before. Some of her best customers in the Las Vegas days had gone down on her. She loved that, too.

On her honeymoon with Frederick, she had suggested a little oral sex, and he had been thoroughly shocked. He hadn't even wanted her on top. How quaint. The lover she was about to dump was a little more inventive, but he was too old, too eager to get his gun blasted.

"Like me, honey?" she gurgled, undulating her ass and letting her thighs open.

"Very good, baby," he grinned. He drew his briefs down his tanned, muscular legs. The sudden view of his naked crotch, his big thick penis angled high, his large hairy balls sent sweet shivers along her body. He hadn't been circumcised. Delicious! The wetness on his all-man knob where the skin framed it said she was sexy enough to draw the clear slickness. He moved closer to her and tensed his cock.

"Ohhh, you bastard," she breathed. She reached out for it and closed her fingers around the shaft. The feel of a hot, rigid cock, after two weeks of going without, tensed her clitoris. She was just over her period; she hadn't even touched Tracy for a week, and she was dying for cock!

She'd had herself sterilized at age twenty-five, so there was no more worry about getting knocked up. She wasn't the domestic kind of broad, never had been. She was a mercenary bitch; she admitted it and lived with it.

His hands went to her breasts. He unhooked the tricky little pink bra. When she was turned on good, like now, her tits didn't sag. She was proud of the way they firmed out during a sex bout. But she did need support most of the time, and with her tits shaped forward, she was much more appealing.

"I'm glad you're a tittie man," she giggled, watching his fingers roam over her thirty-eights.

He smiled and steered her toward the nearest loveseat. Good! He was going to play with her a while before he got it in her. The nice preliminaries were almost as delicious as the nitty-gritty.

Moving her down to his left, he circled her soft shoulders and let his right hand drift to her crotch. She spread her thighs, curving her pussy up and out, feeling more juice ooze from her cunny. His spicy male aroma and the view of his thick eight-incher made her shudder.

"Long time without, eh?" he murmured.

"Oh, you don't know, honey!" she lied easily. She didn't really count the fun she had had with Tracy or a finger orgasm the night before.

"Good," he chuckled. He caressed the nyloned inner planes of her thighs. She sneaked her left hand to his cock, playing her fingers up and down the shaft lightly. Ohhhh, damn! She knew already it would be a good tight fit in her cunny.

As his hand drew sweet thrills along her legs, he lowered his head toward her breasts. Shivering, she curved her right tit toward his mouth. Her brown, swollen nipple ached for kisses it was her most sensitive one. His tongue shot out, touched her spire of flesh, and slid around it.

"Ohhhh!" she breathed. "Suck it good, honey."

His lips enclosed the nipple, and his tongue danced on it while he inched spicy tingles from her crotch. His hand settled on her panty-covered pussy. She whimpered and swung her cunt higher. The flood of erotic tingles spread across her loins as she hunched on his fingers. Her clit was erected delectably. She felt her juices leaking through the nylon bikini panties onto his fingers. Oh, he was a real teaser.

"Oh, I love it!" she breathed.

His hand swept out along her opened thighs again, pressing and squeezing. Her need was building richly, deliciously. She hadn't felt so wild for cock for ages! She hunched again, again. His fingers returned to her panties, and he worked his hand down inside them, cupping her swollen mons.

He has wonderful hands, she thought, feeling a finger dip into her cunt.

* * *

Jay was enjoying himself. There was nothing quite like getting his mitts on a new pussy, a real eager broad. Kingdoms had been won and lost because of a hot piece of ass. Not that Melanie was all that good, but she was doing better every second. Her hairless twat was interesting.

He slid his play finger into the pudding, and she moaned, her nipples hardening. The one in his mouth received more sucks and tongue-slides. Her cunny wasn't overly large. It was good and slick, and a little twitch of her labia encouraged his explorations.

"Ohhhh!" she breathed, fastening her fingers in his hair. Her slow hunches were deliciously voluptuous.

He flattened his thumb on her clitoris, finding as he had expected a good development. The little tip of her sex puffed up a quarter of an inch. He rolled it gently, and she shuddered, gasping.

"Don't make me cum this way, honey!"

He raised his head from her swollen breasts. He rested his hand, letting her savor the suspense. Her plump thighs quivered, opening farther.

"Don't you like a nice finger cum, baby?" he murmured.

"Damn you," she breathed happily. "Okay, bring me, honey!"

He pushed his finger in deep, watching the expression on her face. Her head curved back, her tits arched forward, she began to hunch. Her juiced cuntlips wiggled on his hand. She had a delightful hip action her pelvis moved up and down with smooth precision as if she had a prick socked inside her cunny. He wasn't bringing her; she was bringing herself.

He remembered the notation on his file that she had been a very popular call girl with a lot of repeats. He could see why. She had loved her work. A lot of those very beautiful long-legged whores were Lesbians.

Melanie might be, too, considering the appearance and actions of Tracy, the dusky, sexy maid with the dainty ass-wiggle. Well, a lot of wise broads were AC-DC. They worked both sides of the tracks. He didn't give a shit one way or the other. He liked banging a woman who loved her bang-bangs.

She rested for a moment, breathing hard. She was prolonging the fun, building her need. He felt her shivers of delight, watching her swollen tits and her opened thighs. More juice leaked out on his hand, and a very weak twitching inside her vagina tensed his cock. Her fingers tightened on it, and she started her rhythmic jerks again.

She moved slowly at first, then tried to stop again, but she was too far along. Her breath sucked in, her face contorted, her ass bucked furiously. A fierce mewing sound rose in her throat, her mouth opened, and the sofa creaked. He felt the surge of her delight. The quick pounding of her orgasm jerked her legs and arms as her cunny slapped at his hand. Her big tits jiggled.

"Uhhh!" she moaned. "Oh, Oh, Ohh!"

"Cum good, baby," he breathed against her breasts.

She whimpered and finished with energetic little ass-lifts,

her vagina tightening spasmodically. At last, she softened, slumping against him, breathing hard. Her thighs closed, and she squeezed them on his hand. A pleased smile touched her lips.

"Ohhhh, that was good!"

"You needed that, baby," he chuckled, drawing his finger out. He patted her hairless mons and drew the panties down so he could see it better.

"Ohh, you know it!" she giggled, squirming around and pushing a breast into his chest. Her fingers danced along the length of his prick. She cuddled his nuts gently.

"I like that bare pussy," he said, stretching the panties out farther.

"I thought you would," she giggled. "Here, let me take my panties off."

He pulled his hand back, and she drew away far enough to slide the wisp of nylon and lace from her ass and down her legs. She tossed the panties on the floor and opened her thighs, curving her cunny upward. The swollen, wet labia reminded him that he hadn't nibbled any cunt for a long time.

He wasn't sure he wanted to eat Melanie, but he did know he was looking forward to sliding his tongue in Jessica's pussy.

"I had it taken off by an expert," Melanie murmured. "And you know, Frederick never did take advantage of it."

He laughed. "Old-fashioned, eh?"

"You wouldn't believe how square he was, honey," she cooed, returning her hand to his cock.

Getting her to talk about her late husband was what he

wanted, the reason he was here. He cupped a breast in his hand, teasing the stiffening brown nipple.

"Didn't he do you any good at all?" he asked.

"Twice a month or so," she said drily. "Ugh!"

"His accident didn't upset you too much, then," he said cleverly.

"Oh, yes, honey. I did get kind of attached to him, you know..." She urged her breast more snugly into his hand. "Hell, let's stop talking about him. From now on, I'm going to have fun."

He sighed inwardly. Even if she did say something incriminating, it wouldn't mean shit. He wasn't taping it, and judges took a dim view of bugging, anyway. She was going to cash in unless he could come up with something definite, maybe a witness. But they had been alone in the house.

* * *

Melanie smiled to herself. The odor of fuzz was getting stronger. Beyond a doubt, he was an insurance company snoop. She was going to enjoy him, anyway, with his beautiful big prick and wonderful hands. She had a little surprise for him later, too.

I really went off hard! she thought. Too bad he's so damned smart. I'd stick around in New York for a while if I could get more of this. Mmmmm!

"Let's try it on the bed, huh?" she breathed, caressing his cock with more eagerness. Her cunny ached for it. Her whole body ached for another orgasm. That big prick would be good and snug in her cock-hungry twat.

He nodded agreeably. She gave his cock a squeeze, stood up, and moved to the bed. She drew the covers back. She didn't want to get that expensive counterpane messed up with man-cum and pussy juice. The wild pink satin sheets had been put on fresh that morning. Tracy had kidded her about it.

"I think I'm going to get a little prick today, honey," she had told Tracy.

The maid had giggled and winked. They had a beautiful understanding.

CHAPTER SEVEN

Seeing Melanie leaning over the bed, straightening the pillows, her plump ass pointing at him, gave him an inspiration. He left the loveseat and moved up behind her, catching her at the waist and pushing his cock between her stocking thighs.

She uttered a gasp of surprise and started to turn around, but he held her with his hands.

"Ohhh, you bastard!" she breathed, softening and spreading her legs. "I haven't had it this way for ages, honey."

"Good."

She tipped her ass backward. He bent his knees slightly and nudged his cockhead against the juicy, expanded target. She lowered her torso, curving her pussy back and up. She'd had cock from behind, so she knew how to position her body. She turned her head, staring at one of the wall mirrors. It was placed at the right angle so she could watch his cock enter her cunny.

The silky, hot spread of her labia around his knob drew his nuts up tight. He gripped her waist firmly, working his cock a little deeper. She shuddered, trying to hunch his tool all the way inside.

"Ohhhh, pour it to me, honey!" she panted.

He trembled and stroked. He felt his foreskin slip back, felt the luscious yield of her flesh around his cock. Very good.

"Uhhhh!" she breathed, back humping. "That's good cock!"

If she wanted to be explicit, he could too, if talking about it inspired her. "Nice snug cunt, baby," he muttered, giving her a good, hard poke.

"Ohh," she gasped, her legs shaking. Her cunny tightened a little, giving him a fine thrill. He kept his cock pushed in deep and reached forward for her pendulous tits. Cupping one in each hand, feeling the hardness of her nipples, he began to fuck.

* * *

Tracy Taylor, peering into the bedroom from the partly opened door, which Melanie had left ajar on purpose, felt a sweet tingling in her crotch. One mirror gave her a side view of the action. Looking straight ahead, she could see only the flex and pump of Jay's muscular ass. The mirrored image was much more exciting!!

He really knew how to fuck, all right. Two or three long slides, then a rest, with all of his big prick soaked deep. Melanie was getting her enjoys! Her face was twisted, her thighs shaking, her elbows sunk deep in the bed. It swayed a little every time he jammed his cock home.

As soon as Tracy had shown Jay into the living room, she had gone to her room out back and changed into a sexy bedroom ensemble. Melanie had promised her a little fun with the new stud, and she certainly wasn't going to miss it!

She had been having a spat with her boyfriend, a bartender downtown, and she hadn't had a man-fuck for two weeks. She didn't mind putting out for Melanie; they could make it pretty good together. The moment she had dropped by Melanie and Frederick's big house for an interview, she had known Melanie liked pussy. It was a good job, and Tracy had decided she could use a little girl-girl sex. In Hawaii, her home state, she had learned to enjoy Lesbian fun with a long-legged Chinese girl. It wasn't like making out with a guy, but it was better than using her fingers.

Jay was a big handsome stud, and he had a tremendous cock. A threesome might be right on! Tracy had never tried it, but she was eager to experiment. Her outfit consisted of yellow bikini panties and a matching bra, with a shorty wrapper that reached just below her crotch. Yellow looked good on her light-brown body. She had been using the pill for years, and at eighteen, she figured she was a pretty good lay. Several guys had told her so, anyway.

Tracy possessed a very dangerous secret. The night Frederick Welch died with a broken neck, she hadn't been at the movies, as she had told Melanie. She had returned home early, slipped in the back door, and been in the shadows of the lower hallway when she saw Melanie catch Frederick off-balance at the top of the long stairway that wound up to the second story. She had seen the whole thing Frederick's tumble after Melanie had shoved him...

It had occurred to Tracy that she had blackmail material in her possession. Her testimony to the right people could put Melanie behind bars for a long, long time. Well, she didn't want to spoil a good thing or become involved. Melanie had said that Tracy could go south after the house was sold and the big insurance payoff was collected. But till then, Melanie said, she wanted to keep Tracy around.

But it was probably all bullshit. That Melanie was a sneaky, unscrupulous bitch, a murderess. Of course, a lot of hip broads married some old bastard for the money, but helping the husband into the grave was strong stuff.

Well, she wasn't going to try any tricky blackmail just yet. She could wait until Melanie went to Las Vegas. Being in the same house with her while starting her play would be very dangerous indeed. Tracy might be the next victim of an "accident".

Meanwhile, there was fun to be had. As soon as Melanie busted her cookies again, it would be a fine time for Tracy's entrance.

* * *

As much as Jay was enjoying himself, he was keeping his eyes open. He had noticed that Melanie hadn't closed the bedroom door, and with all the mirrors around the room, he suddenly knew why. The maid, Tracy, was peering through the crack between the door and casing. Very interesting.

"Ohh, bring me, honey!" Melanie panted, pushing her ass back farther.

Jay gripped her by the hips and drew his cock out until only the knob was centered in her twitching cunny. He wormed it around on her clit, feeling her shudders of delight, knowing she was dangling right on the edge of her cum. She moaned, urging her rump up and out.

It was time. He oozed his cock in hard, giving her a heavy bull-hunch. The press of her ass-cheeks on his groin was very delicious. She whimpered, her rump shook, her vagina fluttered, and he felt the ripples of her cum-joy twist her lush body. A mewing sound broke from her throat, and the beats of her joy were swift and lively.

Her legs gave way, and he followed her down as her belly struck the edge of the bed. He jabbed a few more times. Above Melanie's moans of fulfillment, he heard a faint gasp from behind him. Tracy was staring and staring at the scene on the bed, her dark eyes shining. She was unaware that he was watching her via a mirror.

"Uhhhh, ohhhh!" Melanie moaned, relaxing. Her legs and arms trembled with the shakes of her aftermath. He unsheathed his cock, turning so Tracy could see it well. He grinned at her and tensed his pussy-wet tool.

"Come on in, cutie," he chuckled.

The maid gasped and closed the door. On her bed, Melanie rolled over. She stared up at Jay.

"What's going on? What ?"

"Have your maid come on in, baby," he grinned. "She's been watching. Isn't that what you wanted?"

"Why, that little twitch!" Melanie exclaimed. Then she called out, "Okay, Tracy..."

Jay watched the bedroom door reopen. Tracy wiggled through her yellow bedroom ensemble, indicating she was dressed for fun. Sexy, man. Her brown, smooth body excited his glands; the cute sway of her ass and the pout of her titties in the mini-bra hardened his tongue. Table pussy.

"Can you have more fun with the two of us, honey?" Melanie giggled. She squirmed into a sitting position on the rim of the bed.

"Hell, yes," he grinned. He moved up to Tracy, sliding his

left arm around her waist. He was sure he had guessed right about these two. They had probably worked the threesome thing before. And when there was no stud around, they probably screwed each other. The scene had that kind of odor.

"I'll hit the can, and you two get acquainted, huh?" Melanie giggled, swinging off the bed.

"I like it," Tracy cooed, snuggling in close to Jay. Her shiver, her perfumed nearness, tempted him. Melanie laughed and walked toward the bathroom. When the door closed, Tracy turned and melted against him.

"You're some smooth chick, cute stuff," he said. He traveled his hands from her waist down to her curvy ass. "Bonus baby, eh?"

She giggled softly. "Melanie said I could have a party if I liked you, big man. You're some tiger!"

It occurred to him that he might learn more about the deceased husband from Tracy than he could from Melanie. Only one way to find out.

"How would you like to date me alone sometime, Tracy?" he whispered. His cock was under the hem of her sheer wrapper, pressing into her belly.

"God, yes," she whispered. "Don't tell her. Tell me where I can call you."

He gave her the name of his motel and his room number. She nodded and snuggled in. She held her mouth up. "I never did this threesome thing, honey. Honest."

"You want to go ahead with it?" he murmured.

She giggled, arching her titties against his chest, curving her crotch at his basket. "I'd hate to miss a chance like this!"

Before he could kiss her, Melanie came out of the bathroom. She laughed. "I thought you'd have her titties out, at least, honey."

"He's working from my ass up," Tracy gurgled. She wiggled it in his hands.

He winked at Melanie, keeping his fingers on Tracy's rump, and lowered his mouth to her waiting lips. Her tongue was ready, it met his and they wrestled as her lips opened wide. Her arms slid around his neck. Her shiver of pleasure, the cling of her mouth, hardened his cock. He kneaded the smooth, warm flesh of her butt. She was hungry for it. Her tongue jabbed in his mouth, then drew back. He took the hint and drove his own tongue deep into her throat. Her arms tightened, and she crooned her joy.

Melanie felt a sharp stab of jealousy. She wished now she had sent Tracy out for the afternoon. The little slut was crawling all over him. Their whispering while Melanie was in the bathroom and Tracy's pleased giggles indicated they might be planning something behind the scenes, like a date. Fuzz or not, he was one hell of a stud.

"Why don't you go get all three of us a drink, Tracy?" Melanie said, moving up beside the curvy maid.

Tracy squirmed and enjoyed the embrace a few seconds longer. Their mouths finally came apart. She hunched at his crotch and turned to Melanie.

"Feels so good I hate to put it down," she laughed. "Okay. Be right back." She glanced down at Jay's prick and wiggled to the bedroom door. As she went out, Melanie swept in against Jay, flattening her body close.

"What would you say if I locked her out, honey?" Melanie breathed.

"Hell, it's your party," he said. "You wanted her in on it."

Melanie shuddered. "I guess I can stand to wait! Oh, hell, get that big thing in me again!"

Jay walked Melanie to the bed, and she crawled over in the center, spreading her plump thighs and tipping her crotch upward. Time to give the hostess more prick. Playing with Tracy had hardened his cock. At the moment, he didn't care which of the two he fucked. Melanie was obviously jealous of the maid's youth and freshness.

He crawled between Melanie's opened legs and nudged his cockhead into her wet, swollen labia. She moaned, her face twisted, and she planted her heels in the bed and arched her back. Her cunny twitched a welcome as it slid snugly up around his cock.

"Uhhhh!" she gasped. "Suck my tits, honey!"

He lowered his head to her breasts, positioning his hips and body so she could fuck. She began in earnest. Regardless of her background and her scheming mind, she knew how to skin a prick. Hunch, hunch, hunch, rest. He sucked a nipple in his mouth, feeling her pussy lips flutter around the root of his cock. Panting, she came up again and again. His knob was hitting deep. Her soft thighs burned against his sides.

She was staring up at the ceiling mirror, getting extra kicks from the reflection. The cock-hungry widow was finally getting what she needed after the sample he had given her earlier from behind. Hump, hump, hump. The pneumatic callgirl who loved her work. She rested again, breathing heavily.

He heard the bathroom door open. Lifting his head from Melanie's swollen tits, he glanced over at Tracy. She was staring, a tray held in her left hand. She had removed her yellow bra and panties and wore only the sheer yellow shorty wrapper. Her titties had a beautiful contouring.

"Ohhhh, sexy!" she giggled, putting the tray down on an end table.

"Don't interrupt me now, honey!" Melanie moaned. "You can screw him after a while... Ohh, Ohh!"

Tracy moved to a loveseat that faced the bed. She sat down, her thighs spread, her lightly-fuzzed pussy exposed. She opened the wrapper so he could see her bare, pointy breasts. Her pussy was expanded, and wetness showed along her crevice. She undulated her ass and stuck her tongue out, wiggling it the way she had wiggled it in his mouth.

Melanie moaned again and quickened her movements. Her fingers raked his shoulders, her eyes closed, and her face began to twist. He was tempted to pin her ass to the bed and make her wait longer, but she was getting into her short strokes, just about to bust her goodies.

He winked at Tracy. She smiled, writhing her pretty ass on the loveseat. Her tongue flicked out again, and she arched her tits forward. It was a good ploy, very exciting. His prick tensed, and Melanie's fierce cry of delight signaled her climax.

"Uhh!" she moaned. "Ohh, Oh, Oh, Ohh!"

Her furious bucking, the quick slides of her shivery cunt around his prick, and the shake of her plump thighs on his ribs gave him a good charge. He wasn't cumming, though. It was all a little too showy and mechanical. He let her finish with oozy slidings. She softened, and her legs dropped. Her shivers of relief and the weak twitching of her vagina tickled his ego.

He sank down on her, keeping his cock buried deep, enjoying the tremors of her legs and arms and tits. He gave her a few slow hunches.

"Ohhhh, damn!" she breathed. "That was a good one, honey!"

"Looks like fun!" Tracy giggled.

He lifted away from Melanie, easing his prick slowly from her puffed, slickened cunny. Crawling backward, he stood at the foot of the bed, his wet, swollen cock angled high. Melanie stared at it, her legs jerking in a kind of after-spasm. Her eyes were still hungry.

"Oh, I need that drink now, kids," she smiled, glancing over at Tracy. She raised up and swung around, sitting on the edge of the bed. Tracy lifted a glass from the tray and walked to the bed, handing her employer the highball. Melanie took the drink in her left hand and extended her right hand to Tracy's crotch. She patted it.

"Feels nice and ready for prick, honey."

"You know it, Mel," Tracy giggled.

"Well, go ahead and see if you can take it, honey," Melanie laughed. "That's a lot of prick!"

Tracy backed away from Melanie's hand. She swayed over in front of Jay. "How do you want me, big man?" she cooed.

He caught her around the waist with his left hand and dropped his right to her cunny. He pressed the soft, puffy flesh and let his play finger slide up into her vagina. It was very slick, silky, and sensuous. He pushed in deep, and she shuddered.

"Please, not that way!" she gasped.

"Are you good on top, cutie?"

"Ohhh, yes!" she breathed, hunching on his finger.

"Let's find out," he chuckled. He drew his hand from her pussy and crawled on the bed, settling down on his back. Melanie turned, watching avidly. Tracy moved onto the bed, quickly straddling him, her olive thighs opened above his angled prick. He spread the halves of the filmy wrapper, taking a warm, swollen tittie in each hand. The little nipples were hard. She shivered as her ass dropped. She fastened her pussy at the root of his cock and squirmed her labia around. The juices from her cunny wet the underside of his cock. Very good!

"Ohhh!" she breathed, shivering.

"Well, get it in, honey," Melanie laughed, peering down in between Tracy's opened thighs.

Suddenly, the doorbell chimes rang. Tracy gasped, and her cute ass stopped moving.

"Shit!" Melanie burst out. She moved from the bed, put her glass down, and moved to the closet. "I'll see who it is."

She found a robe, put it on, and swayed out of the bedroom, leaving the door ajar.

Tracy moved quickly. Her hips swung forward, and she settled her soft, hot pussy on his knob and began to slip it up inside.

"Ohh!" she gasped. "Get me off before she comes back, honey!"

"I thought you liked the scene," he said.

"She's jealous as hell! Can't you tell?"

"Okay, cute stuff. Do you think?"

Tracy whimpered, shoving down hard. His cock oozed snugly upward into her juicy cunt. Her hazel eyes widened, her tits swelled in his hands, her snug vagina twitched voluptuously around his meat.

"Ohhhh, that's good cock!" she breathed, starting to fuck.

Oh, I never had so much cock in my pussy!" Tracy thought, pumping her ass up and down. Sweet shit! I nearly flipped out when I saw Melanie bust her cookies around his prick! I don't want her watching when I cum, though. What I need is a whole night with this big, handsome stud. Alone!

She stroked three times and waited breathlessly. Voices came very faintly from the living room.

Melanie wasn't getting rid of the caller very fast. Good! She snugged her thighs against his body and angled her torso higher, gripping his arms for support. She began to hunch. At every poke, his big knob hit the opening of her womb. Her stretched pussy twitched its delight as she felt the sweet thrills of a climax start along her legs and sweep to her crotch and clitoris.

"Ohh, Oh!" she gasped, arching her titties into his hands. "You're getting my gun, honey! Ohhh, hell! Ohhh, here it comes!"

"Blow a hard one, baby!" he breathed.

She rocked her ass swiftly. Her clit pulsed wildly, her cunny tightened voluptuously. The hard, quick pounding of her orgasm wrenched her whole pelvis! Suddenly his hands dropped from her breasts; he got a firm grip on her ass and began to hunch up. He was going to cum! Her pussy was sexy enough to draw his load!

She felt the heavenly tensing of his prick, the hot swell of his knob. Her pussy tightened again, again, again! He groaned, his face contorted, his cock throbbed. His vigorous drives into her cumming cunt whirled her into ecstasy. She shouted! She felt the bed jiggling and swaying. She slumped forward, mashing her titties into his heaving chest.

* * *

Melanie slammed the front door in the magazine salesman's face and ran toward the bedroom, cursing under her breath. Tracy's plaintive cry of ecstasy said she was having fun already! The little slut! As she pushed the bedroom door open, she saw Tracy crouched above him, her pretty ass still humping. Her mouth was fastened to his mouth, and his hands were caressing her waist and rump. The jealousy she had experienced earlier flamed into a storm.

"Okay, you've had your piece, honey," Melanie said drily.

Tracy raised her head. "I'm sorry, Mel. I thought "

"I know," Melanie said. "You can get the hell out, now."

Tracy's pleased smile faded. She nodded and lifted away. As the maid crawled from the bed, Melanie saw the white, thick man-cream leaking down her thighs.

Something snapped in her brain. I wanted that shot of cum! she thought. I stepped out of the room, and he blasted his load in her young, fresh pussy! The studs always like the young stuff the best. Damn her, I'm going to fire her ass out of here!

Tracy slid off the bed, and Jay followed her. His prick was turning soft, and he had a funny look on his face.

"I'm splitting, too, Melanie," he said.

"Fuck you both!" Melanie blazed. "I can get all the prick I need, any time, without you fuzz!"

Jay smiled coolly. He began to pick up his clothes. "I'll be seeing you later, baby. This was your idea, not mine."

"Get the hell out!" Melanie shouted. "Both of you!"

CHAPTER EIGHT

Jay was relaxing in his motel unit when the phone rang. It was five o'clock, over two hours since his experience at Melanie Welch's home. He was looking forward to his date with Jessica. He had promised to pick her up at eight, and this time, he was sure he was going to give her the full treatment. He would take her somewhere else this time.

"Yeah," he said into the receiver. He had been expecting a call from his attorney, but the voice was soft, feminine, and very sexy.

"This is Jay, isn't it?"

"Right." Not Tracy Taylor's voice. Maybe she never would call. Maybe she and Melanie had patched up their differences. Still, he wouldn't mind giving Tracy another screw. She was a sweet lady, a very cute chick.

"This is Amy Daniels, honey," came the sultry, provocative voice. "You know, Jessica's sister. She doesn't know I'm calling, though..."

He felt a twinge of desire in his groin. "I'm flattered," he said. "I heard you had a steady."

She laughed intimately. "Not that steady, stud. Wouldn't you like to sample younger sister?"

His cock began to rise in his shorts. A vision of Amy danced provocatively in his mind. These young mod twats laid it right on the line, man.

"I wouldn't want to hurt Jessica," he said.

"Hell, I wouldn't say a word, honey. Look, I know you're taking her out tonight. I mean, maybe in a day or two. We could have fun."

"Let me think about it, beautiful," he chuckled. She giggled. "You won't be sorry. I'm a good wiggle."

"Okay, I'll be in touch, Amy..."

The minute he dropped the receiver, he reached down and patted his cock-lump. Another new pussy wanted fucking! Things were looking better all the time. No shy virgin, there she would be hot and experienced. He didn't want to screw things up with Jessica, though.

At seven-thirty, when he stepped out of the shower, his phone rang again. This time, it was Tracy Taylor, and her voice had cozy overtones, too.

"Melanie kicked me clear out," Tracy said. "I'm staying with a girlfriend. Are we going to have that date one of these days, honey? I think I have something to tell you..."

"Sure, Tracy," he said. "I thought you and Melanie got along pretty well."

"We did, for a while. The lousy bitch! That was a good job. I'm gonna get even with her!"

Something started to click in his mind. Thinking about Jessica and Amy had moved him from his purpose. He started remembering. "What do you have to tell me, Tracy?"

"You take me out, and I'll give you the lowdown, honey." Her voice turned cozy again. "That cock of yours sure felt good!"

He laughed. It wouldn't do to push her too hard, but on the other hand, she might have something on her former employer, hot-panties Melanie. He knew he would never dig any information out of the widow. She knew he was "fuzz".

"Nice hot pussy, Tracy," he chuckled. "Give me your number there, eh?"

She did. They chatted a while, and then he dropped the receiver.

* * *

"Come in, Jay," Jessica smiled, her hands trembling. It was just eight o'clock, and he was right on time. He looked so terribly handsome and appealing that she felt a warm glow in her crotch, and her nipples tingled.

"Hey, you look good," he grinned, moving into the apartment living room. "Are we all alone?"

"Yes," she said, feeling lightheaded. "Amy's out on a date, and so is Martha. Would you like to stay here for a while?"

"Sure," he said, turning. He walked up to her and slipped his arms around her waist. "You don't like to go out in public much, eh?"

She shivered. "Well, people do stare at me. But I'll do anything you want to, Jay."

His arms tightened. She shuddered. She knew her sister and mother wouldn't be home until at least one or two in the morning. Amy was still going with John Castle, and Martha had a heavy date with Oscar Stern.

I spent hours getting ready for him, she thought. I do like it here. I can relax better. I want him to go all the way this time! We were just starting at his motel, and then the roof fell in. I'm nuts about him. I dreamed about him all day. I could hardly get my work done.

"Like parking on a side road?" he chuckled, his hands caressing her waist, drawing her in closer.

"Ohhhh, yes!" she breathed, remembering her violent first orgasm with him. She loved having him tease her. Things didn't get quite so heavy that way. It let her relax better.

"I enjoyed that, too," he murmured. He aimed his mouth at hers. She shuddered, her thin bikini panties turning wet in the crotch. She was dressed to go out in case he wanted to take her to some public place, but this would be much cozier. After a while, she could change. She had a new yellow negligee she wanted to show him. She had modeled it a week earlier at a style show and had decided to buy one like it.

His mouth brushed into her eager lips, and his tongue wiggled into her mouth. She slid her arms around his neck, pressing her body tightly to his. The feel of him again, his virile nearness, whirled her senses. He simply couldn't know just how much she needed this!

He's had lots of girls, and I haven't had one guy! she thought wildly. Not all the way! God! My clit is already stiff, my nipples are hard. I'm burning all over!

Jay tasted the sweet hunger of her mouth, felt the press of her beautiful body against him, and his prick started swelling. The bedroom antics with Melanie and Tracy seemed far away now. Instead of an easy former callgirl and a tramp of a maid, he had a woman, a girl-woman hungry for sex, naive, passionate, and very willing to learn.

Easing his hands down to her firm, sweet ass, he cupped the

cheeks and began lifting her miniskirt in the back. She wore a very provocative outfit: a frilly, frothy blouse that curved low in front, shaping her jutting breasts, dark stay-up stockings, and a skirt that showed most of her long, shapely thighs.

His fingers slid under her skirt. He touched the silky, thin panties and felt her shiver of delight, the tightening of her arms. Her tongue snaked across his, her breasts pushed at his chest, and her lips trembled. He touched bare flesh between her panties and the tops of her stockings, pleased that she wasn't wearing pantyhose.

Her thighs opened slightly. She incurved her crotch with more vigor. A tremor ran the length of her beautiful body.

Delicious tingles ran up Jessica's legs to her cunny and spread across her loins. All day, she'd resisted the urge to slip into the restroom in the office and relieve her need, especially after he had called her and made the date. She was almost ashamed of the violent responses he awakened in her body. She didn't want him to think she was some kind of nympho!

He likes it when I cum, though, she thought, feeling his tongue sound the depths of her hungry mouth. And I'm going to make it soon if he keeps doing what he's doing!

Her aching clitoris tensed in her moistened labia, her nipples stiffened in her think pink bikini bra. He hadn't played with her pussy yet. They had only gotten started in his motel. Now his fingers were teasing the flesh near her cunny, and he was playing with her ass. His tongue was drawing the honey from clear down between her legs.

Oh, God! she thought dizzily. I'm cumming already! I dreamed about him all day. My clit tingled when he called, and it's been ready to do its thing ever since! Ohhhh, here it comes! It's like that time in the front seat when he played with my titties, but it's sweeter and deeper!

She twisted her mouth from his, moaned, and panted against his neck. Her ass started moving.

She couldn't keep it still. She was hunching at his basket, faster and faster! The honeyed throbs racked her whole crotch! Beat, beat, beat, beat!

"Ohh, Ohh, Honey!" she cried fiercely.

She floated in a pulsing thrill of fulfillment. Every nerve in her body seemed to vibrate exquisitely. Her clit was pouring a stream of golden bullets at his crotch! She was shuddering and humping like an animal, giving everything she had to give for her big, handsome lover.

"Beautiful!" he murmured, holding her close, dancing his fingers on her quivering rump and cuddling her ass in his strong, virile hands.

"Ohhhh!" she breathed, her legs weakening. "I have to sit down, honey!"

"Right," he said, guiding her to a sofa. She sank down at his left, still in her aftermath, shaky with relief. Her skirt was almost to her ass, and she didn't try to pull it forward. She rested limply, breathing hard.

"That's the kind of kiss I like, Jessica," he said, his left arm circling her shoulders.

"You must think I'm a regular hussy," she murmured. She hid her face against his throat. "If you only knew..."

"I think I know, beautiful," he said. "You haven't been

around much. It's okay, understand? I told you that before. Just be yourself."

She trembled. I have to remember not to be too clinging and heavy, she thought. He wants a playgirl, not a wife! He'll look around and marry a city girl, sure as hell. I'm just lucky he likes me this well. If I could just be the way Amy is with a guy! I watched her screw John, and she made it just a fun thing.

"All right, honey," she said, raising her head.

"You want to play some more here or take me in the bedroom?"

He laughed. "Cut a few corners, eh? I still want to see what's inside that nice blouse of yours."

"I thought you'd like it," she giggled. "I haven't seen what's in your pants!"

Jay sensed she was making an effort to be casual and sophisticated, trying to act a part, and it bothered him. Maybe Amy had something to do with this? There was nothing backward about her style.

Well, this might be the best approach with Jessica until he knew her better. He would play her little game and see what happened.

She's herself when she goes off, man, he thought. No girl can fake that! She shoots both barrels. Wham, bang, boom!

He took her mouth again and lifted his right hand to her blouse. He found the little zipper at the center, hidden by a frill of lace, and ran it down. Her lips opened. He nibbled at the sensual thickness of her lower lip and spread the front of her blouse. His fingers contacted a thin bra, bulgy with promise. She shuddered, her ass restless on the sofa. Her long right thigh pressed into his leg. He inhaled the blend of perfume and girl aroma; his prick tingled and stiffened up along his belly.

"Ohhhh!" she breathed, shivering again.

Her breasts arched out. He released her mouth. She rested her head on his shoulder, breathing unevenly. He looked at her breasts, decorated by the wisp of lace-trimmed nylon. He admired the sweet pout of her nipples against the hug of the bra cups. Terrific pair of tits! He had enjoyed them before, but tonight, he was going to enjoy them more.

The view of her long thighs open invitingly, her miniskirt back far enough to reveal the curve of her pussy, and the pink, lace-bordered panties, moist along the crevice, ridged his cock to full length and stiffness.

Carefully, he unhooked the bra, a front-opener like the other one she had worn, and covered a tanned, firm mound of girl flesh. He squeezed, watching her nipples swell out on their widely aureoled peaks. Her tits were long, coned hills of exquisite allure.

"Ohhh!" she breathed, shuddering. Her lips fastened on his neck, her thighs quivered, her ass writhed. She half-turned her torso, curving her titties forward. She wasn't acting now. She was all eagerness, all go. He had a suspicion he was the first man who had ever played with her breasts. The poor girl was dying for another climax!

Jessica felt more juice oozing from her shivery pussy into her panties. The sweet rise of her nipples in his toying fingers sent more wild shivers down to her crotch, and her clit erected achingly for another cum! She remembered Amy's boldness with John Castle, and she had to show her appreciation somehow, so she reached out with her left hand and pressed her fingers against his basket. He trembled. The size of his prick, the length, and thickness of it under his pants, surged her quaky need higher.

She was starting into another climax!

"Ohh, Ohh!" she cried fiercely, her hips lifting. God! I want that big thing in my cunny, she thought dizzily. I can't pretend any longer! He said to be myself, and that's what I'm doing! I'm cumming again for him, just for him! Oh, it's happening better than before! It's ripping my whole crotch!

Her hips seemed to be filled with coil springs. She was hunching up, her legs kicking, her tits heaving. The sweetness rushed along her thighs and down from her swollen breasts and excruciatingly out to the point of her clitoris. She shouted!

For pounding, golden seconds, the hard pulsing of her climax transported her into a dream. She wasn't using her fingers or her dildo; she was having her orgasm with her big, strong lover! What delight, what heaven! Her clit was shooting hard and fast! It was bursting with passion, exploding, her need rushing from the tip in a sweet flood of erotic joy.

She quieted, slumping back in the circle of his arm, panting her relief, feeling the sweeps of aftermath feed her need and bathe her loins with delectable shivers. Each time she went off for him, the sensations got better!

"Ohhhh, Jay!" she breathed, her hand still pressing into his manhood, the big lump in his pants. "What you do to me!"

"I like it, Jessica," he murmured, cuddling a tit in his cupping hand. "You're terrific!"

She hid her face against his shoulder, remembering too vividly all her years of loneliness, of being called "Stilts" and other ugly nicknames. A rush of gratitude made her eyes turn wet. She couldn't be lightheaded and casual about something as strong as this, couldn't treat her first big sex experience with a man the way Amy treated hers.

Guys had been chasing Amy since the age of thirteen, and she had started scoring with them as soon as Martha had taught her how to use contraceptives. Jessica, at twenty-one, had never before had a bare, hot prick in her fingers, let alone in her pussy! It was now or never.

"Take me in the bedroom and give me everything, honey," she breathed, kissing his throat, tears running down her cheeks. "I have to give it to you straight. I've never done it, ever!"

"Hell, I know that by now, beautiful," he said, fondling her achy breasts. "Are you sure about it?"

"Yes, yes!" she breathed, her voice shaky. "Please!"

* * *

Amy, cooling her heels in the dimness of the hallway while peering into the living room, shook her head disapprovingly. Jessica was getting way too heavy with it, telling him she'd never had a screw. How ridiculous!

Amy had cut her date short, telling John Castle she had a headache. She had become so curious about what Jessica would do with Jay that she had left a window in her bedroom unlocked and the screen unhooked so she could slip in at the rear of the apartment.

She had arrived just in time to see Jay bring Jessica's titties out and watch the exciting finale. Jessica really went ape when she got her jollies! Amy could hardly blame her sister, though. He was one beautiful hunk of a man, and that lump in his pants looked right on. What a horse!

When I called him, he sounded interested, Amy thought, watching Jessica recover from her climax. I'll get him out one of these nights and show him what a hot pussy really is. Jessica watched me get a little the other night. Now, I want to see her take a cock.

Amy remembered the time she had come home early from school and caught her parents having a little. Seeing Jeff's car in the driveway, she had slipped quietly into the house. She had been fourteen then. Martha's laughter from the master bedroom had drawn Amy toward it. The door had been open, and as she had peeked through, she had seen Martha just mounting.

The vision of Jeff's cock entering Martha's cunny, Martha's moan of pleasure, and her position above Jeff had excited Amy's glands. Somehow the view of her parents screwing, even though she knew they had been doing it for years and years, had seemed more compelling than if they had not been married.

It had been Amy's first real lesson about fucking. The hurry-up screws she'd had from young guys just weren't much compared to the way Martha worked. Sitting up on Jeff's prick, she had made the fun last and last. Even their sexy conversation had given Amy new ideas. But the most startling thing of all was the way Martha had worked up to a climax with slow, easy strokes, reached her climax with cries of delight, rested a while, and then went after another bang-bang.

Jeff had encouraged her to have as many orgasms as she could. He had been able to hold his shot for over an hour!

Now Jessica was moving into her bedroom, damn it. Amy realized she might have to listen instead of watch. She retreated to her own bedroom, went inside, and made sure the door on her side of the connecting bathroom was locked. She was sure Jessica would use the facilities before she crawled into bed with her big stud.

Sure enough, Amy heard Jessica enter the bathroom and start fussing around. Amy sat in darkness, waiting, her pussy very wet and tingly.

John Castle was okay. He didn't mind taking a good-looking wench out in public, but he very obviously wasn't going any further with it. Some cute city chick in his strata of society would nail him down. Well, she wasn't ready to get married yet, anyway.

* * *

Jay undressed and surveyed Jessica's bedroom. It was large and well-furnished, richly draped. Martha was a very comfortably fixed widow, and she wanted to live in style. Jessica had said she was thinking about getting her own apartment, and she made good money at the Stern Insurance Agency. But the family seemed very close, a tightly knit unit.

Naked, he rested on the edge of the bed, waiting for Jessica to come out of the bathroom. She had turned the lights down very low. He hoped she wouldn't want the room in complete darkness. She had a terrific body, and he liked to look at it.

The door opened, and his cock tingled. Jessica wore a short red nightie that struck her just below the pussy and was slashed in front over her jutting breasts. She stared at his crotch, her lips open. She rushed over beside him and sat down at his left, her head resting on his shoulder.

"Now I'm scared, honey," she murmured, shivering.

"Hell, I understand," he said, getting his left arm around her. She snuggled in, turning her mouth for a kiss. The warm yield of her lips spread open for his tongue, and her hungry little moan swelled his prick. He eased her backward on the bed. She shuddered, her tongue begging for his tongue. He gave it to her, deep and hard.

This is it! Jessica thought, feeling his tongue slide sweetly in her mouth. I asked for the work, and I'm going to get screwed! What a cock! My God! If he ever gets that big thing into me, I'll go out of my skull! I am scared, but I know he'll take it easy with me and do a good job. Mmmmm!

I wanted it the other night; I was all ready to swing. This is better, though, because I'm home and no one else is here and we can have all kinds of fun.

His hand slipped along her waist, under the hem of her nightie, and in on her bare, swollen cunny! She had freshened it in the bathroom and dabbed away the excess wetness, but now more juice was leaking out. Her breasts, in the sheer red nightie, felt a foot long!

The feel of his fingers on her puffy flesh as he explored her crotch, pressing it gently, sent wild shudders the length of her body. Her very first man touch her pussy! Her hips lifted, her thighs began to spread, her clit erected into delectable stiffness. It had a new sensitivity and ached fiercely. She ached all over, from her mouth to her nipples to her crotch.

His fingers traced a fiery pathway up and down her crevice. She moaned into his mouth, her tongue plunging swiftly. His play finger went slowly in. As many times as she had imagined how it would be, as many times as she had done it herself, the sensations were still more delightful than she'd dreamed they would be! His closeness, his mouth on hers, the spicy male aroma, and the knowledge that a man wanted her made the difference!

His finger-end grazed her clitoris, and she shuddered, her thighs jerking. Her breath caught, her mouth came unglued, her hips lifted. The thrills of rapture shot along her legs, up over her belly, and out to the point of her clit, so sweet and swift and good she moaned fiercely.

His finger slid in deep again! The slick, juicy plunge into her unpricked cunt was starting her cum!

"Ohh, Ohh, God!" she cried. "Ohhhh, oh. Ohh!"

Her hips caught a swift up-and-down motion as the heaven bunched in her crotch. Her breasts arched upward, her nipples expanded and hardened, a flood of quick hard beats rampaged through her loins, and her cunny twitched around his finger! The sensations rocked her senses!

Suddenly the end of his digit hit very deep, a very sensitive place she often struck with the knob of the dildo. Her pelvis exploded! The cum-joy went on and on and on! She was bucking and kicking the way she had on the sofa, but now she had something to hump on!

The quivering of her vagina she sometimes felt when she had an orgasm with her dildo was becoming a sweet, wild clenching. The spasms rocked her into dreamland. For long seconds, she floated and sailed, cocooned in sensual heat, every nerve in her being responding to his overpowering maleness.

Floating down from her feathery cloud, she hugged him close and panted against his neck.

"Ohhhh, Jay! Ohhhh, mmmmmm!"

"Beautiful," he murmured. His finger wasn't in her now. He was holding her swollen pussy with his whole hand, squeezing her flesh, drawing the last little shivers of relief from her crotch. Her clit felt a whole inch long, and her legs still shivered with the aftermath. No orgasm had ever been so thorough, so utterly shattering! She was limp with joy and exquisite alleviation.

Oh, I never knew I could ever cum so big and furious for anyone, she thought dizzily. He makes it real; he makes it far, far out! I'm nuts about him! I knew he could do me good; I just knew it! And he hasn't even got his cock in yet...

CHAPTER NINE

Stretched out comfortably on the bed at Jay's left, Jessica spread her long thighs and watched his right hand slip under the hem of her nightie. It settled on her crotch, and his fingers began to play along the inner zones of her legs. Her swollen titties were out of the top of her nightie. He raised up on his left elbow, and his head lowered toward her stiffened nipples.

His prick touched her right hip. She shuddered and reached for it. As her fingers went around the pillar of maleness, all wet on the knob, more dampness oozed from her cunny. After her wild finger orgasm, she had used a towel on her crotch, but it was all slick and ready again. It had never been so puffy! The pink inner flesh was squeezing out past the outer labia. It was a moist red flower between her shanks.

Oh, he was so gentle and careful with her body! He already knew she wasn't a virgin, and she didn't know how to tell him way. Earlier, she had planned to mention an old boyfriend who never existed, but the truth was out, and he already knew she had never been screwed!

Her dildo and what she had done with it time after time began to haunt her. She simply had to level with him, somehow.

Jay's cock tensed as he opened his lips and sucked in a dark, tumid nipple. He was glad she hadn't turned the lamp off. He loved to look at her beautiful body, those long legs and her narrow waist, and her high-rising tits. And what a hot, snug cunny! Sonofabitch!

It tightened around my finger, he thought, feeling her shivers of rising need. Her cunt twitches when she goes off! It happens with older women, but I didn't expect that in a girl so young. I'll have to use more fingers and mouth than prick.

That her hymen was gone didn't bug him too much. Twenty-one-year-old virgins didn't happen anymore. She was very passionate. She had probably broken her maidenhead with a candle or her fingers. She had already told him that her mother had given her plenty of lowdown on sex.

Her fingers gripped his cock, her thighs opened farther, and her nipple swelled delectably in his mouth. Fuck! He couldn't wait any longer. She needed prick in the worst way, and he was hungry for her cunt. One blast would slow him, but he was good for two or three with a girl as hot as Jessica.

"Ohhhh, do it!" she panted, her left hand clutching at his hair.

She was as ready as a girl could ever be. He raised his head, letting her nipple slip from his mouth, and crawled over between her opened, waiting thighs. Her right hand stayed on his cock. She couldn't let go of it. The touch of her trembly fingers swelled his knob. The fierce ache in his groin had to find relief. He had played with her and teased her long enough!

He knew she'd never had a man between her legs. Hymen or not, she was still a virgin! He would break her in to fuck just the way he liked it, an untrained bundle of eager girl. It was almost too much.

*　*　*

Feverish with lust, Jessica released her hole on his big, beautiful cock and angled her legs farther apart. She upcurved her drippy pussy, watching him bring his tool toward her crotch. This was the moment she had waited for since she had first learned how to cum on her fingers! She was going to feel her first prick!

His hips swung down and in, his arms braced his torso, and his huge wet prickhead nudged into her swollen cunt!

The luscious yield of her flesh around his knob, the sweet burn of his sex as it spread her labia, sucked a wild cry from her lips. She dug her heels into the bed and lifted her ass. Her legs jerked against his legs. Her vagina stretched, stretched! For a crazy instant, she didn't think she was going to be able to take it! But suddenly, the knob was slipping, squeezing... deep!

The view of his huge sexy shaft sliding into her cunny, the hot steamy connection, the flutter of her pussy flesh around his cock, and the very first plunge of man into her depths made her moan fiercely.

"Ohh, Ohh, Ohh!"

I've got him! she thought dizzily. He's in me! It's so good! I can't believe it! My cunt is crammed with prick! The head of it feels a foot across. It's reaching clear to my anus! My God! I'm going to get fucked! It's his pussy! He can do anything he wants to with it!

"Jesus!" he muttered, his face flushed.

He liked her cunny! He loved its snugness, the sweet fit

of her flesh around his! The honeyed thrills were chasing everywhere!

Slowly, he began to fuck.

Control, man, control! He thought, sounding her shivery vagina with his rigid cock. Make it last! It's such a good tight cunt I'm going to blow my mind!

He would show her more about how to place her ass and legs a little later. Right now wasn't the time. She was getting her first cock the poor girl had waited too many years for it, and he was reaching in far enough. Slide, slide, slide, wait! Her cunt twitched, and she moaned, her fingers digging at his shoulders, her face twisted with passion.

The sweet, hot cling of her cuntlips around his cock, the squish of his bit nuts into her swollen mons every time he stroked, and the luscious jab of his huge cockhead against her depths sent such furious thrills across her loins and out to the tip of her clitoris that she shouted her joy.

"Ohh, Ohh, Jay!"

"Cum, beautiful!" he panted, resting, flexing his big prick in her twitchy cunt. "Cum good and hard!"

"Ohh, yes!" she cried wildly. "Screw me hard!"

His cock came almost out, and she looked down at the pussy-slick, swollen shaft of his maleness. He was making her wait golden seconds, building her suspense. The curve of his strong, tanned body between her long shanks, the black hair around his big, drawn-up nuts, and the big cock waiting to drive into her depths drove her crazy!

Suddenly he shuddered, his knob tensed, his face contorted, and she knew he was going to cum in her cunt! He groaned, his hips drove down, his huge cock jammed into her quaking vagina, and he began to screw with wild, studlike abandon! A wild curse escaped his lips as the huge hot cock went in and out, in and out, faster and faster. He was bulling her cunt, sliding her ass along the bed with his virile thrusts!

She screamed!

Her tits pushed higher, her nipples hardened, her clit stiffened, and she felt the dreamy hot thrills chase along her shaking thighs to her achy crotch. His big nuts were slapping at the cheeks of her ass, and his big knob was pounding at the opening of her womb, trying to slip inside it! A furious clenching and spasming of her cunt whirled her into pulsing dreamland! Beat, beat, beat, beat! Her clit was exploding, and her girly-prick was shooting at his pumping cock!

The delicious tightening of her vagina made her scream again. Each clench of her hungry cunt matched the sweet throbbing of his shooting cock. She was getting his load of cum, her very first burst of semen! His studlike thrusts into her cunt, his bleat of rapture, and the wild shake of the bed matched the hard jungle fury of her own need. She bucked and kicked her legs and hunched upward with all her strength.

We're two animals lusting and straining, she thought wildly. And ohhh, how sweet it is! I never knew what a cum really was till now! That big thing is still sliding; it's pulling the thrills from my legs and tits and mouth and even my anus! Ohh, what a piece of ass! What a fuck!

He stopped humping and slumped down on her, panting into her hair. The sweet quivers of his relief made her own aftermath doubly intense. She was sharing her joy! What a difference it made!

"Damn!" he muttered, hunching again. "That is good pussy!"

"Ohhhh, God!" she cried, tears in her eyes. "I'm glad, honey! I want it to be the best pussy you ever had!"

She swung her long legs across his ass and squeezed. She arched her tits up against his chest and hunched her cunt, feeling a river of juices leaking from it down around his cock, dribbling toward her anal crevice. What a luscious, close, sexy sensation! She finally had some rich man-cream mixed with her cunt-juice!

Sonofabitch! Jay thought, feeling her long thighs tighten around his butt. She's a tigress! Her cunt actually clenches when she goes off! I can't believe it. Most chicks can't do that till they've had years of practice! Jessica is just naturally that way unless she's been practicing on her fingers or a candle or something else. I don't give a shit! She's got it for me, anyway. That cunt is the best I've ever had. Amazing!

* * *

Amy, peering through a crack between Jessica's bathroom door and the casing, shivered and slipped her right hand under her miniskirt. She cupped her tender, pantied cunny, her clit burning, her nipples erect in her decorative bra.

The scene on Jessica's bed flamed in her mind. What a stud he was, what a cock! Jessica had barely been able to take it! But she had it now. Her pussy was filled with it, and she had got her first gush of jism.

Amy realized she would have to stop peeping, though. Jessica would be coming to the can to freshen her pussy and wipe away the man-cum. Amy closed the door very carefully, not locking it, and slipped backward through her door and into her darkened bedroom. Enough light came into the room from the opened window so she could see her way around.

In spite of all Amy had told Jessica about having fun with guys, Jessica was still getting heavy with it. Falling really hard for some stud was the best way to get really hurt! Some chicks had to learn the hard way!

She sure blows hard! Amy thought almost enviously. I thought she was going to buck him off the bed! Well, I liked my first prick, too. I was thirteen, and I went off pretty well for a beginner. But not like Jessica. Wow! She screamed her head off! He likes her pussy, too. He said so. Well, wait till he gets it in me! I'll show him what skinning a prick is all about.

* * *

Jay started to draw his cock from Jessica's wet, quivery cunt, and her legs tightened convulsively, her arms gripping him tightly.

"Ohhhh, leave it in, honey!" she breathed. Moisture showed at her hairline, and an expression of thrall and wonder made her more beautiful than ever. The hungry appeal in her voice humbled him. She had her first cock, and she didn't want to let go of it.

Her legs relaxed, he felt more juice leak from her cunny, and she trembled.

"I'll be back in there, sweetie," he said.

Jessica had never felt so gloriously feminine in her whole life. She was still in a daze of fulfillment. Her nerves were alive, and her body was glowing with a sweet inner warmth. He was above her, in command, his big cock snugged delectably in her flesh. Nothing had ever felt so good, absolutely nothing! She was flooded with his man-cum and how beautiful it was!

As she felt more moistness oozing from her filled, expanded cunny, she knew why he wanted to take his cock out. She was a mess! Perspiration was wetting her forehead and the nape of her neck. She wanted to be very fresh and dainty for him. She had to use the can and quickly.

Her thighs swung out. He lifted away, and she raised her head to watch his half-stiff manhood emerge from her pussy. Ohhhh, how sexy! It was all laved with thick white cream and her own cunty oozings. He rolled away on his back, and she slipped from the bed, wishing she had put towels out for the overflow.

She raced to the toilet door, a whole river of goop running down her thighs. Legs shaky, she slipped into the bathroom and turned on the light. A perfumed aroma touched her nostrils. It was the kind of scent Amy wore, a very musky perfume, and it was very strong.

Well, they shared the bathroom, but a little dagger of suspicion ran through her mind. The door on her side hadn't been entirely closed... She found two towels, laid one out for Jay, and held hers against her puffy mons. She almost hated to lose that precious man-stuff. It belonged up in her cunny! Martha claimed regular shots of jism were better for a girl's complexion than all the expensive face creams in the world. And Martha had gotten it, and she didn't look her age at all.

Jessica pushed on Amy's door. It was unlocked. Shivering, she reached through and found the switch beside the casing. She flicked it, filling the bedroom with light. She uttered a gasp.

Amy sat on her bed, smiling.

Jessica moved through, closing the door behind her. "Oh, you damned peeper!" Jessica breathed.

"You had fun watching me screw John, honey," Amy giggled. "Tit for tat." She stared at Jessica's body, thinly covered by the red nightie. "Was it really good?"

Jessica felt some of her glow fading. She couldn't be really mad at Amy; they were too close. She was simply disgusted. She glanced at the bedroom window, the opened drapes, the unhooked screen.

"You're... awful!" Jessica whispered. "I think I'll have him take me to a motel. You've had all kinds of guys, and he's my first one!"

Amy smiled. "Okay, I'll stay in here and be as quiet as a mouse. I saw him get it in. Some cock!"

Jessica trembled, shook her head, and retreated into the bathroom. She closed the door and locked it. If Amy had to use the toilet, she could go into Martha's bedroom, the sneaky little bitch. Quickly, Jessica began to get herself ready for more fun. She took the nightie off. Jay was naked, so she wanted to be naked, too. But something had gone out of the evening. She wasn't really alone with him now. Amy would be listening.

* * *

Jay took his ear from the bathroom door and returned to Jessica's bed. His hearing was very keen. He had heard voices, and he had caught most of what had been said. He and Jessica weren't alone in the apartment, after all. Very interesting. He remembered Amy's looks, her voice on the phone.

He was sure Jessica hadn't planned things this way. It sure wouldn't stop him from enjoying more of her body. A friend of his in Los Angeles was servicing two sisters. They were going the threesome route, all in bed at the same time. Beyond a doubt, Amy would go for it. Well, he would play it innocent-like and see what happened.

Grinning, he wiped his cock on his handkerchief and stretched out on the bed. Even with no experience, Jessica was a tremendous screw. That voluptuous twitching of her cunt was sensational! He had a lot of plans for that lovely, tall lady with a hot mouth and beautiful breasts.

He still wondered who had made the call that had brought the narc agents to his motel. Maybe Amy. No, it was more like Alexa Daniels. She really hated his guts. On the other hand, if it hadn't been for Alexa, he wouldn't have met Jessica. One of these days, he would have to call Alexa. That blonde cunt needed to be taught a lesson.

The bathroom door opened, and Jessica stepped out, the nightie gone. She held a towel in her hand, and her smile looked a little shaky. But her figure was just as appealing. His prick began to re-stiffen.

She stared at it and rushed to the bed, swinging down at

his left and snuggling up close. She handed him the towel. She felt warm and smooth, and she smelled fragrant and utterly desirable.

"Sorry I was gone so long, honey," she breathed. "I have to tell you this, Jay. Amy sneaked back home, and she's in her bedroom right now."

He acted surprised. "Hell, that's okay, beautiful. We can still have our fun, eh?"

"Ohhhh, I hope so!" she gasped, her long right thigh burning into his leg. "I guess we should have gone someplace else."

"Next time," he grinned. "I have a special spot in mind."

"Oh, God, Jay!" she breathed. "You're so good to me!"

He does want me again, she thought, shuddering. I don't care how much Amy hears! I know she wants to screw him too. It's written all over her. But I saw him first, and he got to me first, and I'll be such a good fuck he won't ever want another girl! Amy can get her fun someplace else!

His hand slipped along her belly toward her crotch. She drew her thighs apart, reached for his big hard cock, and held it tightly in her fingers. He was up hard again, and the sweet thickness of his manhood sent shiver after shiver along her body. She knew she would never, never get enough of that big, wonderful prick!

His fingers played along the sensitive inner zones of her thighs, coaxing sweet shivers from her cunny. Her clit hardened, her nipples peaked out again, and the wild hunger began to flame in her pelvis. She arched her swollen breasts toward his mouth. He half-turned, resting on his left elbow, and his head moved toward her ager, tumid nipples. She watched his tongue come out and lave a tender tit-peak, coiling around a nipple.

"Ohhhh!" she breathed, lifting her ass. "I love it!"

He trembled, his hand settled on her cunny, and his lips finally took her spire of tit-flesh. His gentle sucks enlarged her breasts even more. She had never seen them so big! They were ready to burst like ripe melons. She felt more pussy juice oozing out on his pressing fingers, and she hunched. His big cock tensed in her hand as his tongue flirted sweetly with her achy nipple. She felt the dreamy, hot tingles of her need spread down to her crotch. She hunched up again and again!

The shock of finding her sister in her room was all gone now. Everything was hot and cozy again. The fierce craving for his cock seemed stronger than ever. She was going out of her mind! She could hardly bear this suspense! Well, he was used to playing with and fondling his dates, and he wanted to enjoy her body, but she had waited so many years for what most girls started having in their early teens; she was simply frantic!

"Ohhh, Ohh!" she panted, feeling a quick, luscious bunching of passion in her crotch. Her thighs quivered, her ass wiggled up and down. Dreamy tingles fled from her tits to her clitoris. She was swept into another climax! There was no way she could delay the fun. It was rushing along her legs and out to her tensing clit.

She shouted as the hard, swift throbs of delight wrenched her loins. Throb, throb, throb, throb! Her clit was pouring honey on his hand, her legs were kicking and jerking with the beats of her joy, her tits were heaving, and every nerve in her pussy was exploding!

It wasn't like having his cock sliding and jousting in her cunt, but it was sheer heaven. Her clit had never shot such a salvo of thrills!

"Ohh, Oh, ohhhhhh, honey!" she panted, driving her pussy at his hand.

"Beautiful!" he murmured against her trembling breasts. "You cum real good for me, Jessica."

"Oh, I want to cum for you all night!" she panted, caressing his big hard cock. She was surprised at her boldness, but she had to tell him. Cumming for him was just the utter end, a real trip! Wave after wave of exquisite relief bathed her crotch, her tits, her ass.

He was so considerate. He knew a hot girl could cum time after luscious time, and the more often she went off, the better he liked her. Tears of gratitude wet her eyes again. He was just too much!

Amy, resting in her bed, wearing a sheer yellow nightie, slipped her right hand down to her tingling pussy. She hadn't played with herself for a long time, but she knew she had to tonight. She wished she had let John get in her panties before she had developed her "headache". What she had really developed was a hard ache for Jay's cock. What a tool he had!

Jessica's loud cry of delight, penetrating both bathroom doors, had brought a lot of juice from Amy's cunny. Her clit was ridged and tender it needed relief in the worst way. She placed a finger on each side of her point of pleasure and began to hunch up. She loved to move her ass when she was getting her jollies.

A lamp glowed beside her bed. She drew the hem of her nightie back with her free hand and took time to admire her brown, opened thighs and her titties rising up inside the cling of the sheer yellow nylon. She was a pretty classy dish, all right. When she ass-wiggled down the street in a miniskirt, her tits jiggling in a tight, revealing blouse, men really stared.

Seeing her for the first time, Jay had stared, too. He wanted her pussy; all right, he surely must know that some girls were hot in the sack. He had halfway promised her a date, too.

Oh, I wish I could screw him tonight, she thought. Martha is out getting her prick, and Jessica is getting her fun, and I'm left out. That's a new twist. I should call John and have him come to the apartment, and we could all four have a swinging party. But I'm getting a little tired of John. I want Jay between my legs. Ohhh, shit!

Her hips worked faster. She arched her crotch L up, spread her swollen, wet labia, and looked at her "little boy in the boat." The tiny pink nub of her sex was really up there tonight. She stroked a finger across it and shuddered. A few more tickles, and she would blow her cum. Ohhh, it was going to be a good one, too. Seeing Jessica get her first cock had really charged her batteries.

A faint, cozy laugh from Jessica's bedroom sent pangs of envy through Amy's being. She was glad for Jessica but horribly envious, too. He was probably teasing her toward another climax.

Amy shuddered. Very carefully, she inserted the tip of her

little finger in her urethra, pushed her thumb on her clitoris, and felt the sweet thrills fly across her loins. The urethra bit was something she had learned by reading a very interesting book about sex. The opening was almost as sensitive as her clitoris. Ohhhh, yes! Love that pussy!

Her tits swelled in her nightie, her dark nipples poking at the clinging fabric. She weaved her shoulders. She liked to watch her breasts jiggle when she was about ready to cum. They firmed up really well. She didn't play with her tits; she saved that pleasure for when she was out on a date. The cunt was where the action was, anyway.

She paused, breathing unevenly, letting the thrills eddy through her crotch. There was one thing about using her hand: she could delay her fun as long as she cared to. Most guys didn't really know how to play with a pussy; they were too anxious to get the cock in and start pumping.

She wiggled her little finger and teased her clitpoint again. Zingy! The thrills were really heavy. She flexed her beautiful legs, resting again. Waiting and waiting for the goodies was almost as dreamy as getting them! She imagined Jay had his hand on her cunt. Ohhhh, yes! Ohhh, now! She couldn't hold back any longer! The thrills shot up her legs and out to her clit, and the first hot pounding of her climax sucked a moan from her throat. Her hips flew, her fingers working right in rhythm with her pulsing fun, fun, fun! It was the best finger-fuck she'd had for ages!

CHAPTER TEN

Just as Amy finished her orgasm, the apartment doorbell rang.

She swore and lifted her hand from her pussy. She slid off the bed, ran to her closet, found a robe, and put it on. The damned bell rang again before she could leave the room and run out into the living area.

The laughter in Jessica's room had stopped. It was very quiet. It was nearly ten o'clock. Who the hell would be ringing their doorbell at this hour? Some drunk, probably.

She snatched the door open and felt a mild surprise. A very pretty blonde in a tight sweater and miniskirt smiled and looked Amy up and down.

"My name is Alexa Daniels, honey," the girl said. "I work with Jessica. Is she home?"

"No," Amy lied easily. "She's out with her boyfriend."

"That's funny," the blonde said drily. "I see his car sitting out in front. I have something important to tell her."

"You'll see her tomorrow, cutie. Run along and spook somebody else."

The blonde's lip curled. "You getting some of his cock too, honey?"

"Go screw yourself," Amy snapped. She closed the door and locked it. A cynical laugh came from behind the thick panel. Then things turned quiet.

Amy sank into a chair, hoping the noise hadn't interrupted Jessica's good time with Jay.

* * *

Jessica was starting to crawl above Jay when the doorbell sounded. She trembled, hesitating. A curse formed on her lips. Well, Amy would handle it. But somehow, the delightful trance she was in began to slip away. Too many lousy intrusions! She needed to be totally alone with Jay.

"Come on, play around, beautiful," he smiled, his hands reaching for her titties.

She trembled and lowered her steaming pussy to his crotch. His big prick burned into her belly as her labia settled on his nuts. Suddenly, she heard Alexa Daniels's voice. The blonde bitch! She had no business being there! She had never visited the apartment before.

"Oh, I'd better see what's going on!" Jessica breathed. "God, I hate this!"

"Hell, don't worry, Jessica."

She nodded and moved away, her need fading. Even knowing Amy was in the apartment, listening was bugging her. She walked to her closet, found a robe, and left the bedroom, anger boiling up inside her.

* * *

"Say, this is some spread," Tracy Taylor exclaimed, gazing around the interior of Jay's motel room. It was Wednesday evening.

"Two beds," he grinned. "We can take our pick."

She giggled, squirming against him. His cock was starting to swell. He knew he would have to give her more of it. He was sure now she had information about Melanie Welch that could damage the widow's insurance claim, but the price was a sex party.

The night before with Jessica hadn't ended too well. He had a date with her for Friday night, so he could finish exploring her beautiful body then. Amy's sneaky return to the apartment hadn't done Jessica much good, and then Alexa's visit had finished things. He was positive now that Alexa had made the anonymous call to the fuzz that had brought the narcs to his motel. The clever blonde slut was really sore.

And to make things worse, while he had been dancing with Tracy at the Downtowner, a place she had insisted on visiting for drinks and fun, Alexa and Chanelle, the receptionist at Stern Insurance, had spotted him. Alexa would tell Jessica, of course. That fucking blonde was like a pox she was everywhere! Luck hadn't been moving with him for a week.

Tracy pushed herself closer, holding her head up. Her frock was very revealing, cut low in front and short in the skirt. The chocolate-colored moons of her breasts were nearly out of the bodice of her dress. She had downed three martinis, had rubbed around on him during the dancing, and now was ready for sack fun.

"Did you like the way I topped out, honey?" she breathed, incurving her crotch.

"Hell, yes, baby," he chuckled. He passed his hands across her undulating ass. She shivered, and her tongue came out, wiggling.

"Boy, Melanie really flipped when she found out you went off in me!" Tracy giggled.

"Yeah," he grinned. He hiked her skirt up and caressed her pantied rump. She shivered, hunching at his basket.

"Jesus, let's get in bed, honey!" she breathed. "I didn't get half enough cock yesterday."

He began to lower her panties.

* * *

Jessica tried to watch TV, but her mind wasn't on it. All she could think about was Jay, and she wouldn't see him until Friday evening! He had business to take care of. The memory of him leaving the apartment the night before put an ache in her crotch. Well, he had promised to take her to a very special place next time, where nobody would be fouling up the works.

He screwed me, though, she thought, trembling. He shot his passion in me, and I went out of my mind. Ohhhh, I wanted him to stay all night!

The phone rang, and she left her chair to answer it. Martha had gone to bed early, and Amy was at a movie.

"Yes?" she said, hoping it might be him.

"Alexa here, honey," came the answer.

Recalling the trouble she had caused before, Jessica almost dropped the receiver. Her bright mood vanished.

"What the hell do you want?" Jessica asked.

"Just thought I'd tell you," Alexa said dryly. "I was at the Downtowner a while ago and saw Jay with a cute Hawaiian-looking chick. He took her to his motel. They're there now, honey. He's probably got it in her cunt already." The words ended in a sneering laugh.

"Oh, you filthy bitch!" Jessica cried, slamming the receiver down. Waves of jealousy ran through her. It couldn't be true! Alexa was just trying to stir up more trouble.

Twenty minutes later, Jessica parked her car near Jay's motel. His Dodge was parked in the slot, and lights burned in his motel unit. Shivering, she left her car and walked quietly along until she was in front of his door. It was a quiet street. Hating herself, she tiptoed up to the entrance and put her ear to the door.

A girlish laugh came from inside, followed by Jay's chuckle. Oh, he was entertaining a chick! Business, indeed! She wanted to stick around a few moments, but auto lights approaching drew her back to the sidewalk. She hurried to her car and crawled in behind the steering wheel, her hands trembling, an awful coldness in her loins.

Oh, damn him! she thought. He said I was his girl, and now he's playing with some other chick. I shouldn't have come here. I hate Alexa for calling. I wouldn't give her any, and she's been on my back ever since. Ohhh, hell! He doesn't really want to go steady with a tall freak like me.

Tears in her eyes, she started the motor and burned rubber, getting away from the curb.

* * *

Amy flattened her body against Jay's big, strong frame and shivered with anticipation. They were dancing in a small cocktail lounge in Tribeca. She had had several highballs, and she was riding high. It was Thursday night.

That afternoon, she had caught Jay at his motel, and he had agreed to take her out. She wasn't too surprised at his willingness after she had learned that he and Jessica had fallen out. Poor Jessica! She had hardly started dating him, and she figured she owned him. Well, all was fair in love and war. She was curious, though.

"What did happen between you and Jessica, honey?" Amy murmured. They were in a very dimly lighted corner of the small dance floor. She urged her heating pussy at his basket.

"She found out I was with some chick last night," he said. "It was a business deal, but she wouldn't believe me."

"Hell," Amy giggled. "She ought to know a big stud like you gets plenty of pussy."

He laughed. "She is a pretty special kind of girl, though."

"Right," Amy said. "I can't knock my own sister. I shouldn't have slipped back home the other night when you two were having fun. I'm sorry." She added. "You know, you're the first boyfriend she ever had."

"I wish I could make up to her some way," he said.

"I'll try to talk to her, honey," Amy murmured. "She's nuts about you, and she really needs plenty of loving."

His arm around her waist tightened. She knew she looked sexy in her basic black frock, slashed at the throat and short enough to show her legs and ass where they counted.

"You're quite a bundle, Amy. Young and exciting."

She trembled. "How long are you going to tease me, honey? Let's go somewhere and swing, huh?"

Jay felt a sweet, surging ache in his nuts. Amy had the same kind of voluptuous appeal that Jessica possessed. They were both tigers, except that Amy conformed to the more standard pattern of prettiness, a little over average height, bold, and sure of her sexiness. The new generation sex symbol. Men had been ogling her since the age of eleven, or maybe younger.

He felt good. He had spent half the day on the Melanie Welch business, taking testimony from Tracy Taylor. The attorney hired locally by his company was presenting the evidence to a judge in Superior Court, and it was a cinch that the coroner's jury verdict would be upset by the findings relating to the death of Frederick Welch. Melanie wasn't going to get her big chunk of loot.

He could clear out in a few days and return to Los Angeles. The only big disappointment was Jessica. That bitch, Alexa Daniels, had blabbed about Tracy. Sure, he had enjoyed screwing Tracy, but he hadn't wasted himself. She had produced the evidence he needed.

Another thing was turning out well, too. The city didn't want an expose in court of how their narcs had pulled an illegal raid. They were going to settle. His attorney was working on it now.

As he opened the motel unit door and watched Amy wiggle in ahead of him, his cock began to harden. She wanted action, and she was going to get action. No interruptions this time. He realized he should have brought Jessica to a place like this, out of the city's center. Too late now. The younger sister wanted some hot sliding dick.

"Oh, I like this!" Amy gurgled, twitching to the big bed and perching on the edge. Her beautiful thighs were open so he could see where her long dark stockings ended and her yellow panties began.

Some of her actions and mannerisms, even the tone of

her voice, reminded him of Jessica. His cockhead swelled and tingled. She leaned back on the bed, opened her legs farther, and writhed her curvy ass.

"I like that," he grinned.

She giggled, closed her thighs, and ran over to the radio. She found a music station she liked, then turned and moved toward him. She twitched her body in time to the rock rhythms oozing from the radio. The movements of her shoulders opened the slashed bodice, giving him flashes of firm, bare titties. He had already realized she wore no bra.

Standing in front of him, she undulated her ass and long, beautiful legs. Her tongue flirted between her thick, sensual lips. She giggled.

"Well, do something about what you like, honey," she breathed. Her hazel eyes shone as she glanced down at his cock-lump.

He caught her around the waist with his left hand and pulled her in close. He slid his right hand up to her temptingly concealed breasts, jutting forward almost as far as Jessica's sensational titties. He inserted his hand between the halves of her bodice and found a bare, warm mound of girl flesh, the nipple already pointy.

She trembled, her lips opened, her tongue waited. He took her mouth hungrily, fitting his fingers more comfortably around her left breast. Her tongue daggered into his mouth. She curved her crotch at his basket. Her right arm snaked around his neck. She moaned as he teased her nipple. He let her use her knowing tongue. She was very good with it.

Stroke, stroke, stroke rest. She hunched at his hard-on. Her thighs spread, and she shivered again. She was not putting it on, either. Her uneven breathing through her nose, the hot mash of her lips into his, built his need. Sonofabitch! She was as hot as Jessica, but she knew more about what to do with her body. The liberated teenager, hungry for cock.

Amy shuddered, feeling sweet hot juices dribbling from her cunny. She'd had a clit hard-on ever since she met him two blocks from the apartment and crawled into his car. He was more man than she had ever run into, so much man her whole body ached for him.

She had one big advantage, too. She had seen him in action, watched him slide his big prick into Jessica's pussy, and heard her sister's wild cries of delight. But he was even sexier up close. It was more than just stealing Jessica's boyfriend. He was turning her on as she had never been turned on before!

Sisters sometimes went for the same guy. Sometimes they screwed the same stud, too. A model she worked with now and then was getting her prick on a regular basis from her older sister's husband.

As she stroked her tongue in Jay's mouth, she remembered a conversation she had had with her girlfriend.

"You mean to say your sister knows her hubby is screwing you, Anna?" Amy had asked.

"Sure, it was her idea, honey," Anna had laughed.

"Sweet shit! Can't your sister give him enough pussy?"

"No. She'd rather have him getting his strange stuff from a gal she can trust. I don't live with them, honey. I have my own place, but when I get good and horny, I go over to visit, and we have a little swinging party. Fun!"

"You mean a threesome?" Amy had inquired.

"Oh, sort of," Anna had giggled, winking. "Look, I'm not Lesbian. There are a lot of ways to go, though. It puts new life into her hubby, and she gets even more when I'm not around..."

Amy finally eased her mouth from Jay's mouth and breathed against his throat.

"Will you please get me in bed, honey? I'm dying!"

He squeezed her tit and released her. They began to undress.

* * *

Jessica sat alone in the apartment, dressed for bed. She was trying to read a book, but nothing was sticking in her mind. All she could think about was Jay. He had called her at work that morning, and she had told him what she had heard the night before at his motel.

She was still hurting. If he considered playing the field as "business", she couldn't bear the thought of playing second fiddle. Amy hadn't helped the cause by sneaking back to the apartment, either. It was all a mess, of course. Amy was out again, but not with John Castle. She had left the apartment alone. The thing with John seemed to be cooling.

God, I wonder if she's with Jay? Jessica asked herself, throwing the book on the floor. When she wants a guy, she goes right after him, and it's very clear that she wants to get in his pants. Ohhhh, hell!

She hadn't spent nearly as much time with Jay as she had hoped to. He hadn't done a lot of things she had craved. That bitch Alexa had shown up at the very wrong time!

Amy told me not to get heavy with an affair, she thought dully. Easy for her to say! She's been screwing for years, and I've had only one good piece in my life! Ohhhh, damn! I'm all turned on. I guess I'll have to use my dildo again...

* * *

Down to his briefs, Jay watched Amy toss her frock over the back of a chair. In her yellow bikini panties and black nylons, she was wildly appealing. Her titties had a delicious thrust, her waist was as slim as Jessica's, and her ass was just as curvy.

He moved over and drew her down on the edge of the bed at his left. In the soft light from one lamp, she reminded him again of her older sister, a dusky, lithe animal.

She snuggled out, outcurving her breasts, sliding her right arm around his neck. Even her perfume and girl aroma reminded him of Jessica. Damn. He'd have to stop comparing them. He slipped his right hand down between her dusky thighs, and she spread them eagerly. Her left hand went to his cock-lump. He touched her panties just as she settled her fingers on his thinly covered manhood.

"Nnnnn!" she breathed, hunching. "God, what a prick!"

He felt the wetness on her thin panties, and his cock stiffened. He played his fingers along her dusky thighs. She shivered, her hand working inside his briefs. She bit her fingers around his prick, and her hips worked slowly up and down.

He returned his hand to her cunny and pressed it hard. She shuddered, hunching faster.

"Nice hot pussy," he said teasingly.

"Ohhh, get it in me before I cum, honey!" she breathed. "Please!"

"Don't you like a finger-cum, beautiful?" he chuckled.

"Yes, but I like it inside better!" she panted.

He liked to tease the young, bold ones and make them wait for their goodies. She didn't turn on as fast as Jessica. She'd been around. Keeping his hand on her pantied cunt, he dropped his head down to her swollen titties. She shivered, curving them toward his mouth. Her agile hip-lifts were quickening.

"I'll get it in soon, beautiful," he murmured, wetting a pointy nipple with his tongue. "A nice, sexy chick like you needs to be appreciated."

"Ohhhhh, you bastard," she breathed. She worked her hand inside his briefs and fastened her fingers around his cockshaft. Her shudder of pleasure tensed his cock. He imitated her move, sliding his finger past the band of her panties and down on the wet, warm pussy. It was delectably swollen, the crevice drippy. He played with her labia, and she arched with more vigor. Her ass had a beautiful, uninhibited freedom.

"Mmm!" she whined, gripping his prick harder. "Ohhhh, shit! I'm cumming, honey!"

He sucked a nipple in his lips. Her shoulders wiggled, her thighs quivered, and her free hand dug at his shoulder. She began to buck furiously. He felt the sweet shakes of her delight, the tremors of her joy. A low whine of pleasure turned into a fierce squeal. Her legs jerked as actively as Jessica's; she reached her peak and shuddered through it, her last humps squishing her pussyflesh against his palm. Just as she drifted down from her cum-joy, he slid a finger into her cunt.

A few faint tremors rewarded his first testing of her cunny. She had a good, snug vagina. It would be fine and tight around his cock. She whined again and softened as his lips released the pointy tip of her tit.

"Ohhhh, shit!" she breathed, her cunt very juicy around his finger.

"Does that mean it was good?" he chuckled.

"Ohhh, right on!" she sighed, writhing her ass.

Damn! she thought, floating sweetly in her aftermath. No wonder Jessica is nuts about him. I get beautiful vibes. But the best part is, he's a tickler and a teaser. He wants me to have fun. I cum real hard for him. Love that big, hard cock! When he gets it in me, I'll blow my mind!

His hand came out of her panties. He stood up and drew his briefs down. She stared at his huge, rigid prick. She had seen it before when he'd been entertaining Jessica, but knowing it was now her turn for it made such a big difference.

She sank back on the bed, her heels still on the floor, her legs opened. She hunched invitingly, more wetness leaking from her turned-on cunny.

"Take my panties off and see what it looks like, huh?" she giggled.

"Feeling is believing," he grinned.

She shuddered. She adored a man who could be relaxed about the best thing there was, who didn't start getting heavy. John wasn't bad, but he sure wasn't in Jay's league. She was afraid she might be the one getting heavy. He made her body just sing.

He and Jessica had a fight t, she thought. I'll get all the goodies I can while he's in town. He'll be going back to Los Angeles one of these days. But I don't want my sister to find out. I really don't want to hurt her.

"You won't tell Jessica about this, will you?" she said.

"Hell, no, beautiful." He leaned above her and reached for her panties. She trembled and lifted her ass, watching him slide the wisp of nylon from her loins. She closed her legs until the panties were free and then spread them way out, lifting her cunt upward.

Even she was surprised at the swollen condition of her plaything. The lips were puffed way out. Her wet coral inner labia were pushed forward farther than she'd ever seen them. The stinging ache in her clitoris spread along her legs and up to her puffy breasts. No man had ever made her so eager for cock!

"How does it look, honey?" she breathed, hunching again.

He smiled, and his tongue shot out. "Good enough to eat, baby."

"Please screw me first," she breathed. "You're an awful pussy teaser."

He moved around the bed, stretching out on his back. He placed a pillow under his head. She turned quickly, shaking with anticipation. He wanted her to top fuck!

That's my very favorite position, she thought, staring at his huge, uncircumcised phallus. The knob was wet and ready for cunt. He had a tremendous pair of nuts. He was so much man her clit was already tensing for another goody shot.

"Ohhhh, damn!" she breathed, straddling him with her thighs and arms. She lowered her burning crotch, easing her dribbling, leaking cunny to his slanted cock. The touch of his man-flesh against her cunt sent wild shivers through her loins.

"You like it up there, beautiful?" he murmured, reaching for her breasts.

"God, yes!" she gasped. Her slicken labia flamed against his sex. His hands molded her tits, coaxing her nipples into sweet stiffness.

I'm the one who always teases the guys out of their minds, she thought wildly. Now he's doing it to me! Sweet shit! Nobody ever made my pussy ache like this! My "little boy in the boat" is yelling for a cum! Ohhhh, oh, ohhh, he's yelling louder and louder. Ohh, here comes my cunt!

CHAPTER ELEVEN

Amy felt the hot rush of her need. She tried to twist her hips forward and fasten her pussy on his cockhead before she hit her peak, but she was too late! The stabbing pangs of her joy racked her crotch, her cunt started to pour its sex honey, and she dropped down on him, hunching at the hard underswell of his huge burning cock. Her ass bobbed, her cuntlips mashed into his phallus, and the dreamy hard pulses of her cum sucked a wild squeal from her throat.

Jay snatched his hands from Amy's titties and pulled them down to his chest. Her shout and furious hunching brought a grin to his lips. She was really busting a good one! The touch of his prick on her cunt had brought her goodies. She was grinding her pussyflesh at his cock, her legs jerking, her heavy breathing filling his senses with victorious elation.

"Ohhh, Oh, oh, Ohhhh!" she wailed, still humping and bouncing like a young jungle animal. It lasted a long time for her. Beautiful responses and lively motions. When she finally softened, her silky cunt mashed to the slant of his prick, he reached down and cupped the shivery cheeks of her curvy young ass.

"Very good," he breathed, tensing his cock.

"Ohhhh, God!" she breathed. "I wanted it in!"

"Well, raise up and get it in," he chuckled. "I like the way you cum."

I wish to hell this was Jessica, he thought. Amy is a pretty plaything, a hot and dainty swinger, but I can get all of those I want in any color, any size. A few drinks, a few dances, and then sack-time. Shit. I've seen too many of them. Tomorrow I'm going to see Jessica and try to put a ring on her finger!

Amy lifted her wet, swollen pussy. She slid it forward and centered it on the big, hot cockhead. A new kind of fierce craving swept her crotch. She had skinned a lot of pricks; she'd had her fun with a lot of guys, but Jay was very special.

There's something about him that draws the goodies harder and better than anyone ever did, she thought. And I haven't even screwed him yet! I figured it would be really fun to steal Jessica's boyfriend. It is! I never knew I'd feel like such a cheat, a dirty conniver. I do adore my sister, and if she finds out I'm fucking him, it will just kill her!

No matter how good his prick is, I can't do this to Jessica!

She shuddered, settling her cunt back on the big hard underswell of his cock.

"Jay, I have to tell you something," she panted.

His fingers stopped moving on her ass. "Say it, baby."

"You sort of wish Jessica was here instead of me, don't you?"

"Hey, what is this, Amy?" he asked.

"Well, you two really hit it off," Amy said, her pussy leaking more eager juice. "I don't know what happened on your first date, but I spied on you at the apartment and loused up the whole program! Then that damned Alexa homed in." She trembled. "Why don't I call Jessica right now and have her drive out here?"

She felt his tremor, a sweet tensing of his cock, and she knew she had hit him right in the nuts.

"Well, I'll be damned," he muttered. "You mean that, baby?"

"Yes! If she doesn't want me around, I'll just split."

* * *

Jessica moved from her chair in the living room and walked into her bedroom. She looked at the place where she'd had so much fun with Jay, where she had felt her first hard prick. The memories were so sharp and vivid that she shuddered, and her right hand went to her tingling pussy. Tears of anguish welled up in her eyes.

She turned and ran back to the main room and sat down beside the telephone.

I don't care how many girls he's screwed, she thought. I need him! I'm going to call his motel. Just as she started to lift the receiver, the instrument rang. She snatched it out of the cradle, her heart thudding. Maybe it was him!

"Jessica?" came Amy's voice. Jessica sighed and felt miserable. No such luck! But she wondered what her sister wanted. She was out on the town. She might even be with Jay. She knew all about screwing!

"Yes," Jessica answered dully.

"Look, Sis, I have a great big nice surprise for you," Amy said brightly. "That is, if you're over, you're mad at Jay."

The mention of his name sent a wild tremor along her body. Then, another thought seized her. "You're out with him, aren't you?"

"Not the way you think, honey. Now listen..."

* * *

Jessica parked her car at the motel in Northtown, seeing Jay's car in the slot right in front of the door to number eleven. Half an hour had passed since Amy's startling telephone call. Jessica had showered and fixed herself as provocatively as she knew how. She wore a tight blouse, cut low in front, a miniskirt, very thin undies, and long sleek nylons. Her head was spinning wildly. She couldn't believe she was there. Her pussy was already wet and tingly. She couldn't believe her own sister had set up a date for both of them!

It was crazy; it was awful and dirty, but it was one way out for two girls who were both nuts about one big, sexy male animal. A threesome!

I've watched her screw; she's watched me screw; I guess it won't be too bad if we do it right out in the open, she thought, moving out of her car. God! I need him! I'll do anything to get him between my legs again!

She moved up to number eleven and knocked on the door. Her hands were shaking, and her thighs felt weak. Her conscience said no, but her tingling clit and achy nipples said yes, yes!

The panel swung inward. Jay stood there in his trousers, a wide smile of welcome on his handsome face. He looked so good she was utterly speechless. He took her arm, steered her inside, and closed the door. She heard him put the chain on, and then she saw her pretty sister sitting on the edge of the bed in a pair of lacy yellow panties.

"Well, hi, honey!" Amy smiled. "Don't look so shocked. It's real. Sure, I sneaked a date with him, but he wants you. Understand?"

Jessica sagged into a chair, her head spinning wildly. Her miniskirt was back to her crotch, but she was too dazed to slide it forward. Things were happening too swiftly. The whole thing still seemed incredible!

"Jessica, I'll cut out if you want me to," Amy said.

"No!" Jessica cried. "You're prettier than I am! I don't see how you could... do this..."

She knew some girls who were teaming up with one guy. It was happening due to an awful man shortage, but it was supposed to be a really fun scene. But she was a freak, a long, tall girl who towered high in the air. Amy had the body and looks the men went for!

"I'll go to the potty, and you two will have some fun, huh?" Amy giggled, rising from the bed. "I'm glad you want me here, Jessica. He really is your guy."

As the bathroom door closed, Jay sank down on the arm of Jessica's chair. His left arm went around her shoulders. The wash of achy need that swept her crotch was so sweet she opened her thighs and curved her pussy up. Things were all crazy and mixed up, but the feel of him reassured her. She lifted her head for a kiss. His left arm tightened, his right hand went to her frothy blouse, and then his mouth was burrowing into her hungry, spreading lips.

His tongue wiggled voluptuously into her throat as his fingers began to undo her blouse. Ohhhh, it was just delicious! His hands were on her body again, his tongue was sliding in her hungry mouth, and her clit stiffened, tingling with each plunge of his sexy probe.

Oh, I love it, love it! She thought wildly. I adore Amy for getting us together again. I want him to fuck her, too. I can't be that selfish! She can easily find other guys, but I've found only one, and now he's pulling that luscious heat from my titties and mouth and cunny!

She felt the blouse come apart and felt his fingers slip out to the peak of a jutting, thinly covered nipple. She whined into his mouth, arched her breasts forward, and felt her ass writhing in the chair. Every love-starved nerve in her body responded to his overpowering maleness. Having him back after thinking she had lost him made her hunger all the sharper.

Oh, I'm glad I didn't use that dildo, she thought dizzily. I'm going to have the real thing, his big hard prick!

Gently, he stroked her breast and then located the opener on the bra. As it came apart and his warm fingers claimed a swelling tit, she shuddered and whined again. The sugary thrills chasing down to her crotch and along her thighs had never been wilder! Her clit burned and tensed, more juice leaked from her cunny, and her nipple in his fingers stiffened delectably.

His tongue stroked as it had before, like a prick sliding in a cunt. Her arms wound around his neck, her breasts arched out farther, her ass began to move up and down, up and down, creaking the chair-springs. He was doing it to her again! Without even touching her pussy he was pulling the heaven from her sex-starved body!

She couldn't hold back, couldn't delay her rushing tide of need any longer! All of her secret wishes, her dreams about him, congealed into a rich tide of expression. She was getting her gun off!

She hated to lose his tongue; she wanted more and more of it, but she had to shout! The heaven lanced along her shaking thighs, across her pelvis, and out to the point of her flexing clitoris. Her breasts seemed to swell out two feet! Her ass went crazy!

She tore her mouth from his and uttered a fierce cry of fulfillment.

Beat, beat, beat, beat, went her cunt! It was tightening! It was writhing as if it were filled with his big hard, driving cock! She was a lusting bitch in heat, pouring her passion out for her big, handsome lover! Her clit exploded!

"Ohhh, Ohh, Oohh!" she shouted wildly. "Ohh, honey, right on! Amy thought, shivering. He's getting her fun-gun popped already! Wow! She really yells when he bangs her pistol! Sweet Jesus, my cunt is on fire. It needs another cum!

She waited in the bathroom until Jessica finished her cum. She opened the door at last and stepped out, filling her eyes with the sexy vision in front of her. Jessica's breasts were out of her bra and blouse, hard and long, like dusky melons. Her lips looked puffed, and her panties weren't even off. He had given her a tittie-play cum, one of the very best kind!

"Sexy," Amy giggled, swaying over to the bed. She was tired of wearing her panties, which she had put back on before Jessica's arrival. But she hadn't wanted to look too well-screwed. In fact, he hadn't got his cock in her yet! After she had called Jessica, he had pussy-played her into another twitchy orgasm with his skillful fingers. He knew every little sensitive zone in a girl's pussy. He was just too much!

Jessica floated back to earth after her delicious pulsing climax, suddenly aware of Amy sprawled prettily on the edge of the bed. Amy's warm smile, the excitement in her eyes, seemed somehow right.

She got Jay and me back together again, Jessica thought. I owe her, I really do! I don't feel wrong about having her here now. She can help me have more fun with Jay! She didn't have to call me. I watched her screw John Castle, and she watched Jay screw me. We might as well do it right out in the open.

She looked up at Jay. "It's my sister's turn now, honey."

He grinned, his hand still cuddling a tingling, swollen breast. "Is this really okay with you, Jessica?"

"Yes!" she breathed. "I really mean it. We're both stuck on you. We should be able to share you!"

"I won't argue," he smiled. He glanced over at Amy. "Will you please take those panties off?"

Amy giggled and stood up, slipping her yellow wisp of nothing down her legs. Jessica had never seen her sister's pussy so tumescent it was a swollen pink-creviced flower between her thighs. It had never looked that way when she had been screwing John Castle. Her titties were bigger, too.

We both turn on big for him, Jessica thought. She's had a lot of guys, but it's easy to see she's crazy about him. I know her too well. I want to see him get it in her and make her cum!

Jay leaned down and murmured in Jessica's ear, "I'll be back, beautiful."

She trembled and nodded. She couldn't blame him for wanting Amy. She was deliciously sexy, her dusky thighs wide open, wetness glistening between her expanded cuntlips. He lowered his trousers. The view of his huge swollen prick sent sweet shudders along Jessica's body. It seemed larger than ever! Having two hot girls was exciting him more than ever!

Both times she had been with him, there had been interruptions. He still hadn't gone down on her; she hadn't sucked his cock, and they had tried only two positions. As he walked toward Amy, Jessica struggled to her feet and began to undress. It was all a crazy kind of dream, different than she had imagined, but in some ways even more compelling.

Amy was more relaxed and playful. She didn't tie up in knots. They could all have wonderful fun together!

Jay moved in front of Amy. She stared at his cock and fell backward on the bed, wiggling her ass, spreading her thighs even farther apart. He leaned forward, a hand on each side of her, his hips lowering.

"It is all ready for cock, baby?" he asked banteringly.

"God, yes, you animal!" Amy exclaimed.

"Let's see if it's going to fit in there," he chuckled.

Jessica could hardly believe her ears! "Ohhh, haven't you screwed her yet?" she gasped.

"Noo!" Amy said, her legs shaking. "We wanted to wait till you got here, honey, to see if it would be okay with you."

Hands trembling, heart pounding, Jessica removed her blouse and bra. She unhooked her skirt and let it drop. Still in her bikini panties, still a bit backward in this new experience, she moved around so she could see Jay give Amy his cock.

With his feet braced on the carpet, he lowered his head to Amy's upthrusting breasts. Her heels left the floor, and she pulled her legs forward and gripped them with her hands behind the knees. Her crotch lifted as his big sexy prick came in toward her cunt.

His back arched. His lips took one of Amy's stiffened dark nipples. She shuddered, her pretty face twisting with lust. She urged her drippy cunt higher. Shaking with envy, Jessica moved so she could see better. His head lifted from Amy's stiffened nipple, his big wet cockhead nudging into the sexy flower of her cunt.

"Mmmm, Ohhh!" she whimpered as her pussyflesh stretched around his glans. "Get it in!"

Jessica felt more wetness oozing from her swollen pussy into her thin red panties. The vision of her sister's cunt expanding for his cockhead sent wild shivers through her loins. He pushed. Amy's thighs trembled. She winced. Her head rolled from side to side. Slowly his big phallus squeezed into her cunny.

"Mmm, ooh, God!" she wailed. Her ass lifted as he hunched. The huge pillar of man-flesh went out of sight. Amy's head turned back, her breasts arched high, and her thighs jerked. Her arms flopped on the bed, and her belly fluttered.

I know how she feels! Jessica thought. It reaches so far!

Amy couldn't believe she was taking so much cock! Her cunt was crammed with prick-meat! As hot as she was, his knob had hurt her just a little on the journey into her depths, but it was all there now, and the pain was turning into voluptuous shivers of savage intensity.

I'm camming! She thought. I never went off so fast in my life! Ohhh, I never had so much cock!

Here comes my goodies! Sweet Jesus!

Her clit pulsed, her cunt fluttered in a way it never had before, and then she was sweeping to her erotic summit! Wham, bang, pop! Her loins were responding in a different manner, her pussy trying to clench on his huge prick!

"Come, baby, come!" his voice urged. "Break it big!"

The heavenly pounding of her joy rocked her into dreamland. She was kicking and squirming with the beats of her fun! Rockets went off in her crotch. She shouted and bucked! Sometimes, she liked to count the sweet spasms that gripped her loins when she went off, but she was beyond all that. It was happening too swiftly and deeply. Even her anus puckered with the furious intensity of her climax.

Her legs dropped, and she panted in relief, but then the balming washes of the aftermath were so good she wailed with joy again.

"Ohhhh, oh, ohhh, honey!"

I was never screwed like this, she thought, caressing his shoulders. Just one big shove into my cunt, and I blew my wad! God! No wonder Jessica is crazy about him. So am I! I went off good on his hand, but his cock is ten times better!

Suddenly his prick emerged from her twitchy cunt. She whimpered and clutched at him, wanting it back in. The pussy-wet bigness of his shaft was the sexiest thing she had ever seen.

* * *

Martha Daniels rested comfortably on the motel bed, her

thighs opened, two pillows under her head. Oscar Stern, her current steady, was stretched at her right, his hand caressing her swollen cunny. They had been in the motel nearly an hour, had enjoyed several highballs apiece, and after all of the nice preliminaries, they were getting down to the nitty-gritty.

This was her fourth date with him. They couldn't be seen in public because he was married, and any scandal would hurt his business. His wife was a shrew, but she owned half of his prospering insurance agency. A divorce would just about ruin him. Anyway, he wasn't going to marry an old woman, no matter how good she was in the sack.

Martha didn't care to marry again either, but it hurt her a little to realize that he had never mentioned it once. He would never be able to take care of her in bed on a steady basis, anyway. One good sex session a week was about all he could stand. He was fifty-five, and he could hold back for hours, but he was good for only one shot. After he went off, he was finished!

Oh, he was a real gentleman; he had wonderful hands and a hungry mouth. She would probably date him again, but the news was wearing off. She would have to locate another stud.

And whenever she thought of someone else, it always turned out to be Jay Romero. There was a real man. Of course, he was much younger than she, but a lot of guys this age appreciated an older, experienced woman. Ever since she had met him, the first night he had dropped by the apartment to pick up Jessica, she had been dreaming about him. The lump in his pants was tremendous!

Both of her daughters were nuts about him, though. She

didn't stand much of a chance against such competition. He would want a girl he could show off in public, someone young and sexy.

She was glad Jessica had finally found someone.

The poor girl really needed prick and lots of it. Many times, Martha had heard Jessica's bed creaking in the small hours of the morning. That dildo of hers got plenty of use. Amy didn't have to worry she had been screwing for years. But she wasn't inhibited by thinking of herself as too tall.

"A penny for your thoughts, Martha," Oscar murmured, pressing his fingers into her tender cunt.

"I'm thinking about that nice cock of yours," she smiled, reaching for it. If he'd known whose prick she was dreaming of, he wouldn't have liked it.

Her hand crossed his arm. She touched his penis and felt it start to harden. Her fingers closed on it eagerly. His play finger slid juicily into her cunt. She trembled and hunched up. Her vaginal membranes tightened. He shivered.

"Man, you sure can do things with that," he breathed.

Martha was proud of her active, educated cunt. Years before, in Chicago, her mother had given her instructions about pleasing a man. She had learned a few more things on her own, and she had passed her knowledge along to her daughters. In her book, there was nothing wrong or dirty about sex, and she had tried to implant that idea in the minds of Amy and Jessica. A pussy was something to enjoy, with a man or without. She had even told them how to masturbate. Both had well-developed clits. If they didn't have fun, it was their own fault.

Having sex with a man was much more delightful, though much more exciting! Feeling a real prick was a whole lot better than humping on a dildo.

She wiggled her ass on the bed and pushed her cunt towards him again. Oscar trembled, his prick stiffening in her fingers. His thumb went to her tumid clitoris, already swollen from recent playing and kissing. The tender swell of her sex button was nearly half an inch long when she was really hot, erected, and tingled, sending sweet thrills across her pelvis. The first time Oscar discovered it, he had gone off prematurely.

"Uhhhh, that's good, honey," she breathed. "You haven't been there for a long time!"

"I've been tied up, and my wife is getting suspicious," he said.

"Is this the last time, honey?"

"Hell, no, Martha. You're terrific. I'll work something out."

She had heard it before. Men liked her pussy and her big firm tits, but in a place like New York, the big shots didn't show up with unmarried women, at least not in her age. Now and then, some married directors escorted a young untied gal. It was happening more all the time, but she was past that time of life.

She had tried to tell Oscar he was just fun for her, but somehow, it always got a little complicated. Her lovers felt obligated to her. It didn't matter she could locate another middle-aged lover.

She giggled reassuringly. She might as well enjoy him while she had the chance.

"Kiss my tits and make me cum, honey," she breathed,

caressing his cock. "Don't worry about anything. We'll just have a good time of it, huh?"

He nodded eagerly. He was off the hook. Besides, she thought, when she went off, she was going to dream about Jay Romero.

* * *

Jessica watched Amy slide from the bed and wobble toward the bathroom. Amy's cum had brought a lot of juice from her pussy, and she needed a cleanup. When the door closed, Jay moved over to Jessica.

"Damn, you're beautiful," he breathed, his arms sliding around her.

Just the touch of him made her dizzy with yearning. His big cock settled against her belly, his chest mashed into her swollen breasts. Her head tilted, her mouth opened for his tongue, and she got it, thick and warm and sweet. She clutched at him, surges of achy need gripping her loins. She was back where she belonged, and she couldn't blame Amy for wanting him too.

His hands slipped down her waist to her ass, pressing and squeezing. Her clit was a hot little dagger. Every time his tongue stroked her throat, her clitoris tingled, and her nipples hardened. Seeing him stick his big, hard prick in Amy's cunt and knowing she would soon have the same wonderful sensation drew a hungry moan from her throat. Her pussy was puffing out. More wetness oozed into her panties.

She mashed her crotch into his groin, aware that he was guiding her toward the bed. A delicious weakness made her legs shake. She sank down on the edge of the bed, still taking his tongue. His right hand opened her long thighs, and he began to play along the tender inner flesh. She moaned again, her wild craving so sharp and urgent she was already inching toward her climax!

Oh, he was an artist with his fingers! As they teased inward near her cunt she curved it up and out, wishing she had removed her panties. He liked her in them, though. They had all night to play, and he would soon be inside them or have them off. She reached for his big thick penis, and when she touched it, the honeyed thrills in her crotch grew almost unbearable. Stings of delight bladed her loins, and her clitoris erected even more!

I thought I'd lost him, she thought wildly. But my own sister got things straightened out. Ohhh, I'm cumming! I have to cum for him to show him how much I love this and this. Ohhhhh, Ohhh!

The heaven only he had ever drawn from her body began to throb in her crotch. Her mouth broke away, and she groaned fiercely against his neck. The delicious pound, pound, pound of her joy seemed to shoot from the point of her clitoris! She gripped his cock and hunched on his fingers! Each drive of her hips enriched her thrall. She was kicking and bucking the way she had before, in the front seat of his car, when he had first played with her.

"Ohh, Oh, Ohhh!" she shouted. "Ohh, God!"

When Amy heard her sister's plaintive cry of rapture, her clit hardened, and her nipples poked out farther. She was all freshened and ready for more fun, but she had to wait until

Jessica finished her cum. The poor girl needed it so much! She had missed all the dates and backseat pleasures most sexy girls enjoyed for just one reason: she was too tall. But not for Jay.

What a cock he has, she thought, reaching for the doorknob. I never had such an orgasm in my life! That big knob felt like it was trying to get up inside my womb! Ohhh, damn! Just one hard push into my cunt, and I went out of sight! Now I want to watch Jessica take it again!

She opened the bathroom door and shivered. Jessica was stretched out on the bed, in almost the same position Amy had assumed when he had squeezed his prick inside, but she still wore her red, lacy panties. His right hand was inside them, her right hand was holding his huge, swollen cock.

"Sounded like fun, kids!" Amy giggled. She swayed up to the bed.

"Mmm!" Jessica murmured, writhing her hips. "I needed that!"

All three burst out laughing. Oh, it was going to be a beautiful, carefree party. Two hot, eager girls and one big, strong male animal.

CHAPTER TWELVE

"Spread those nice legs a little more, will you, Jessica?"

She trembled and did what he asked. She wore a red mini-bikini, and she was sitting in a deck chair near a swimming pool at a small resort north of New York. The pool was private, enclosed by a high redwood fence. Four days had passed since the motel party with Amy and Jay. He had been very busy, and now they had plenty of time to enjoy themselves.

But the most wonderful thing for Jessica was what she wore on her left hand, a big diamond engagement ring! She could hardly take her eyes off it. He had given it to her three days before, and what with court appearances and trips to Los Angeles, he hadn't had time to cash in on her body. Today was the big day. They both had taken time off, and they had a week to tame their lusts if that was possible.

"Have you been a good girl while I was out of town, beautiful?" he asked, stretching indolently in the chair that faced hers. His eyes teased her body. The big lump in his swim trunks was already making her dizzy.

"Oh, you know it, honey," she breathed, twitching her ass in the chair. "You haven't touched me for three whole, awful days!"

He laughed. "How is that sexy sister of yours?"

"She wants another party," Jessica said, her clit achy for his touches.

"It's up to you two," he grinned.

A sweet shudder raced along Jessica's body. I wanted him to say that! Amy and I talked it all over. If it was possible, she would marry him too! She's gone on him just the way I am! The three of us had so much fun; we girls went off so hard for him; she couldn't wait for more of it!

"Honey, I could call her right now," Jessica giggled. "I said I'd try to talk you into it."

"Great!" he chuckled. "This cabin has an extra bedroom."

"I bet you were thinking about her when you rented it," Jessica laughed.

He came out of his chair, caught her by the hand, and led her inside. "Before you call her, I'm going to show you that you're still my number one girl, understand?"

"I've been waiting and waiting for it, honey," she breathed, flattening herself against him. "Make me cum a dozen times!"

* * *

Very quietly, Amy opened the door of the cabin Jessica had described over the phone. She knew she had the right one because Jay's car was parked in front. A sigh of bedsprings made Amy tremble. She had burned the road from New York. Her pussy was already wet. A red bikini and a pair of swim trunks lay on the cabin living room floor, and the door to what was a big bedroom swung halfway open.

She tiptoed up to the entrance and peered inside. Hot waves of need coursed along her body, and she almost gasped with envy. Jessica was straddled out above him on the wide bed, her ass moving in a sensuous rhythm. She sat nearly upright. His hands were filled with her long, firm titties.

"Drag it out, beautiful," he murmured. "Play around and then have a real big one."

"Ohhh, God!" Jessica cried. "I can't wait, honey! I'm cumming!"

Amy shuddered, reaching under her miniskirt. As she touched her panties, she felt warm juices leaking out on her fingers. Seeing Jessica get the cock, watching her sister hump into an orgasm, was the utter end in voluptuous excitement. Ever since the threesome, Amy had lived in a state of suspense. Nothing like Jay had ever happened to her, and now she was going to share him again!

Suddenly, Jessica slumped forward. His hands came away from her breasts, she mashed them into his chest, and her pretty rounded ass jerked swiftly up and down. The beautiful cadence of her hunches, swift and sure, rocked the bed. Her long, long thighs snuggled against his body began to shake with the fury of her cum-beats.

"Ohh, Oh, Oh, Ohh!" she cried fiercely.

Number five for today, Jessica thought wildly, feeling her cunt tighten voluptuously around his big hard cock. He played with me and kissed me and got his fingers on my pussy and kissed my titties and wham! This is the best, though! This is where the fun is, way up in my cunt! I'm his girl, I'm his long-legged piece, I'm number one! He hasn't gone off yet. I think he's waiting for Amy to show up.

She stopped hunching and rested on his body, the sweet stings of relief washing her mouth, her arms, her tits and thighs and cunt. The burning of her fluttery cuntflesh around his cock was just too wild!

"Very fine," he breathed, caressing her ass and waist.

"Oh, I said I wanted to be the best pussy you ever had!" she panted happily. "I hope I'm getting better, honey."

"Every time," he chuckled. His cock tensed and she shuddered. Her pussy twitched in answer, and her clit began to sting and ache once more. The warm bed of her expanded cunt against his nuts, wet and slick, made her delirious. She would never get enough of his prick never!

"Knock, knock!" came a feminine voice from the doorway.

Jessica lifted her head, shivering. "You sure made it up here fast!"

"I wanted to get here before you wore him out, honey," Amy laughed. She wiggled into the bedroom, looking delicious in a miniskirt, dark nylons, and a blouse that dipped low in front to reveal the upper curves of her breasts. They looked almost ready to fall out. Her nipples showed clearly against the thin fabric.

"Don't worry about that, baby," Jay grinned. "I've got some cock saved for you, too."

Both girls broke out laughing. Somehow, it was more fun with Amy here. It might be wrong and dirty, but oh, how exciting! Jessica wasn't worrying anymore about Jay going whole hog for her sister. After all, she had the ring. Amy was the number two girl.

"Well, undress and join in, honey," Jessica said. "I just had my fifth cum, and I need a little pussy-rest."

Amy dropped her handbag and reached for her blouse. She quickly unbuttoned it and threw it over the back of a chair. No bra. Her titties were swollen into pretty hills, the dark nipples very stiff. Jessica lifted up, drawing her cunt from Jay's big, wet cock. As she fell over on her back to his right, Amy stared at his loins.

"Oh, I don't see how I ever got that in my cunt!" she breathed.

"Maybe you better have him tickle it a while first," Jessica giggled. She drew a towel from beneath a pillow and held it against her drippy pussy. She watched her sister lower the miniskirt. As usual, Amy didn't wear pantyhose, just long nylons, and wild, pink lace-trimmed panties. They were wet along the crevice.

"Looks like you're all turned on," Jessica said.

Amy laughed. "I watched you get that last cum, honey. That really juiced my panties."

Jay smiled to himself, wiping his cock on a towel Jessica had placed for his use. The sisters made a terrific pair. Jessica was much more relaxed with Amy present. Things were still too new for the tall, passionate near-virgin. She was like a young girl of fourteen or so everything was wild and exciting. When the sisters screwed, they tried to outdo each other. Of course, Amy had more experience, but Jessica was the more sensuous. Her clit had more size and erotic development, and her tits were sensational!

His business affairs were all wound up. The statement by Tracy Taylor had nixed the payoff to Melanie Welch, and his attorney and the city were settling out of court. He was going to get a huge payoff. Now, he had ten days of leave to enjoy himself.

His cock tensed as Amy finally slid her pink panties down

her beautiful thighs. He knew she had peeked in the bedroom and watched Jessica buck through her number-five orgasm. The vision had swollen Amy's pussy and peaked her breasts. Very delicious.

"Please let me ride, too, honey!" she giggled, swaying around to the foot of the bed.

He drew the towel from his rigid cock and raised his hips. Her dark eyes flaming with interest, she began to crawl onto the bed. Jessica moved over to give her sister room. Even during the last party, they had never been on the bed together, but they were going for it now. He didn't expect any Lesbian antics, but he had several positions he wanted to try with them.

Jessica watched her pretty sister straddle Jay's hips with her thighs. Her head whirled, and erotic fantasies chased through her mind.

Oh, I want to do it all this time, she thought. He still hasn't eaten either one of us, and we haven't sucked his prick. That other time, we were too busy doing it straight. I want to orgy and have about twenty orgasms! I'm crazy with lust. I'd even go down on Amy if she wanted me to! It wouldn't be wrong with him here!

As Amy spread her legs and curved her pussy down toward his cock, Jessica breathed in his ear.

"Honey, would you eat me right now?"

He nodded and grinned. His tongue came out and wiggled. Jessica trembled, feeling more hot leakage from her swollen cunt. She remembered a photo she had seen of an orgy in progress, one girl riding while the man lapped the other girl. The picture had seemed almost obscene then, but not now!

She scrambled to her knees and gripped the head of the bed, opening her long thighs above his head.

Amy gasped with surprise. Jessica turned her head so she could watch Amy's pussy. It was almost on target! At the same time, she felt Jay's hands gripping her hips, drawing her crotch lower... lower. The sweet burning ache in her cunt just had to be relieved!

Suddenly, she felt the warm, wiggly tip of his tongue slip between her puffed, wet labia. It was so new and sparkly with promise she uttered a cry of delight. Amy moaned, the bed swayed, and his big ball of cockhead began to spread her cuntlips.

"Ohhhhh, it's going in!" Amy panted.

His tongue shot deeper into Jessica's cunt, his lips fastened to her tender flesh, and a gentle sucking drew a fierce cry from her lips. Ohhh, it was happening at last! He was eating her, pulling the thrills from her cunt with his mouth and tongue! Orgy, orgy! His eagerness, the grip of his fingers on her waist, said he liked the taste of her pussy!

Man, that's delicious cunt, Jay thought, drinking more of her juice. It's like rare wine! I've been missing half the fun. I'm the first one to get a tongue in it, too.

He raised her hips slightly and swept his tongue along her swollen crevice to the tumid nub of her clit. Terrific! Her long thighs quivered, and a whine of pleasure reached his ears. The velvety lips opened wider, and the tip of her need stiffened even more. He coiled his tongue around it, and she cried out.

"Ohh, make it cum, honey!"

His tongue stopped moving. He wanted to drag it out for

her just a bit longer. Amy was working her cunt down around his knob. Her little cries of pleasure and the squirm of her ass heightened his enjoyment. Finally, she pushed his prick snugly up in her twitchy cunt.

"Nnn-ohh, Shit!" she yelled.

He flexed his meat. She shuddered and began to fuck. The view of her tits and opened thighs was highly exciting. He was getting it all together now. These beautiful sisters wanted a real party, not just a cock-trade, and he was just the bastard to give it to them.

He began to tongue-tease Jessica's clit.

Oh, he's a devil! she thought, feeling the hot thrills dance across her loins. He's playing with me, making me wait for my next cum! My little gun wants to shoot! Ohhh, I never dreamed his mouth would feel so good on my cunt! Now he's sipping more of my juice. Ohhh, sweet Jesus!

Suddenly she felt two warm, firm tits brushing across her ass. Amy was leaning forward while she fucked, and the close sisterly contact felt utterly dreamy! They were working toward a new kind of intimacy. Amy's hands slid upward and claimed Jessica's achy, swollen breasts.

I just can't help what I'm doing! Amy thought, filling her hands with Jessica's tit-flesh, feeling the nipples harden against her palms. We had never touched each other before, and I don't think I could have if he wasn't here, but I love it! She's ready to cum, I can feel her shivers. Ohhh, I want him to eat me, too! A few guys have tried to lap my pussy, but no one really knew how. Jay does!

Her vagina began to quiver and flutter in a new voluptuous

way! Having his big ham-bone in her snug, slick cunt and rubbing her tits into Jessica's pretty ass was livening her inner cuntal muscles. She humped and shuddered. Ohhh, yes! Her cunt was tightening!

Martha told me my pussy would begin to contract when I found the right guy, she thought dizzily. I figured it was all bullshit. But it isn't! Ohhh, what a blast! Jessica told me yesterday her cunt clenches on his cock when she goes off, and I didn't believe that, either! I do now! I'm turning into a woman!

A faint slurping and sucking sound from between Jessica's thighs and a sweet hardening of Jessica's nipples made Amy hunch again, again. His cock seemed even bigger than before! He liked the way her cunt was responding to his maleness.

All the other guys she had fucked weren't even in the same league with Jay! He could hold and hold his jism; his hands knew every little tender zone of her body; he was just too much! Her clit, daggering into his cock, felt inches long. It was ready to pour honey in delicious spurts. She couldn't wait any longer! She hadn't had any real fun for three whole days. Jessica was ahead of her, and somehow, she had to catch up!

Gripping her sister's tits very hard, she began to buck. The luscious, hot thrills cascaded along her thighs to the tip of her tensing clitoris. Her nipples stiffened against Jessica's rump, and her vagina began to clench in a voluptuous rhythm. She screamed!

Hearing her sister's fierce cry of triumph triggered Jessica's climax. Jay's mouth fastened on her cunt, his tongue stroked deep, his hands dug into her hips. Her nipples peeked out in

Amy's hands. Jessica tried to hunch. She loved to move her ass in the rhythm of her joy, but this time she couldn't. He was drawing the honey from her cunt. The beats were coming slower, but it was happening!

"Ohh, Mmmmm, Ohhh!" she wailed as the pounding delight wrenched her crotch. Her clit was shooting at his mouth, her fun was popping like a repeating cannon. For wild seconds, nothing mattered but the hard, deep, searching throbs of her ultimate joy.

"Isn't he just terrific?" Amy giggled, glancing at her sister in the bathroom mirror.

The girls sat side by side at the motel vanity bench, brushing their hair and touching up their eyes and mouths. Jay had used the bathroom ahead of them. Now, he was waiting for them on the king-sized bed.

"Mmm!" Jessica breathed, winking at Amy. "Shame on you for playing with me."

"Well, I was getting my goodies, and I just couldn't help it," Amy smiled. "And you liked it!"

"I guess we're real whores, huh?" Jessica giggled. She looked at her diamond and shivered. Her freshened pussy was already leaking more fun juice. "Was Mom at the apartment when you left, honey?"

"Yes," Amy said. "She knows where we are, too. I told her." She turned and brushed her lips against Jessica's ear. "She wants to screw him too!"

"Why, that's awful!" Jessica exclaimed, trembling.

Amy laughed softly. "Look, I know he's your guy, but

couldn't you let Martha have just a little of that nice big prick?"

"Well, I've heard about a man taking care of a mother and daughters, but I never thought I'd hear it from you!" Jessica protested.

Amy giggled. "Well, she taught us how to have fun. Maybe it would be swingy to take some in-the-flesh lessons from a real hot woman, huh?"

"I'll think about it," Jessica said. She knew her mother was very interested in Jay, and she had broken up with Oscar Stern. Well, she would leave it up to Jay. She couldn't be selfish with her own sister and mother! He had so much to give.

Martha Daniels, sitting in a deck chair on the small patio at the rear of Jay's rented cabin, watched him dancing with Jessica. It was evening, and a few colored lights glowed around the pool and patio. The afternoon had been almost unbelievable! Jessica had called about two o'clock, and Martha had driven up to the resort, renting a cabin next to Jay's. She had been invited over for cocktails, but the way things were moving, she might just get a little cock to round out her visit.

Jessica and Amy looked delicious in mini-bikinis, and her daughters had insisted that she wear one, too. She couldn't compete with them in youthful prettiness, but the way Jay looked at her, she knew he wanted to get between her thighs. It was obvious he had given both girls a good fucking, and it was just as obvious they wanted more of his sliding prick.

She was so glad that of the two daughters, he had picked Jessica for marriage. She couldn't imagine having a more wonderful son-in-law, and if he wanted a little from her, she would drop over backward any old time!

Amy, sitting at Martha's left, leaned close and breathed in her ear. "Isn't this terrific, Mom? He's going to take turns dancing with us, and he said he wants us to cum with each dance! Fun!"

Martha shuddered. Her clit tingled, and her nipples stiffened in the tight hug of her bikini bra.

"You're rotten!" Martha breathed. "Didn't you both get enough this afternoon?"

"Jessica made it six times, and I went off three," Amy giggled. "She really is hot!"

Martha laughed, more tremors of achy need heating her crotch. She had almost refused to drive to Rockford. The idea of joining in with her sexy daughters was almost shocking. She had never indulged in a threesome, let alone a foursome! Young people nowadays have a different outlook, and girls are doubling up on dates more and more. It was the in thing.

"I hope you two haven't been screwing each other," Martha said, finishing her highball.

"Oh, don't be mid-Victorian, mother," Amy laughed. "We don't go that far with our fun."

Martha shuddered again, her eyes now glued to Jessica and Jay. They were no longer dancing. Their mouths were locked, Jessica was squirming her cunt at Jay's basket, and his hands were kneading her bikini-covered ass. Her long thighs spread, and her rump moved with more vigor.

"Oh, she's about to cum!" Amy giggled, also gazing at her sister.

"He should have it in her," Martha breathed, her whole body aching.

"He's an awful teaser," Amy breathed. "Ohhh, look! Jessica's getting her goodies right now!"

Martha's head whirled, her cunt twitched. She had never seen anything quite so provocative! Jessica's pretty, rounded ass was a blur of erotic movement. She had never looked so startlingly beautiful, her long, lithe body shaking and squirming in rhythm with the beat, beat, beat of her cum-thrills. She was a young savage, catching up on all the fun she had missed in her teens. She had her man now, and she was giving him every ounce of her beauty and passion.

Their mouths broke apart, her head curved back, and a wild cry of fulfillment rang around the enclosure. Her last hunches were furious and dramatic. Martha had told her daughters to be active in a sex scene, and Jessica was doing her thing!

At last, she stopped thrusting at his crotch, and he led her back to the chair she had rested in earlier. She sagged down, her long thighs open, still breathing heavily.

"Oh, you really got me good that time, honey!" she gasped, gazing up at Jay. Her beautiful, swollen tits were nearly ready to pop out of her halter. A line of wetness showed along her crevice where the bikini panties hugged it.

"Great," he smiled. He looked over at Martha. "You want to dance now?"

"You know it!" she breathed, her whole body aching sweetly.

"Rub it all over him, Mom," Amy giggled. "Then it'll be my turn!"

Martha moved to her feet, her legs already shaky. She had

never screwed or played in front of anyone in her life. The whole idea was awful but terribly provocative! She melted eagerly into his embrace, and he steered her to an open area near the pool's edge. The touch of his big, strong body sent wave after wave of furious need through her loins. Her big, thinly sheathed tits pillowed into his chest as she fit her crotch against his cock-lump. She loved to dance; the music was soft and dreamy, but she had never danced this way, knowing the dance wouldn't end until she got her fun gun banged! And right in front of her own daughters, too!

"How can you put up with me when you already have two girls?" she murmured, fitting her cunt mound against his groin. "I'm about a dozen years older than you."

He chuckled, gripping her waist tightly. The hard lump of his cock made her shiver. He brought his hips in closer.

"Hell, I've dated many women, Martha. Terrific!"

"Mature?" she whispered.

"No, and I'm really curious. If you're as hot as your daughters, I'll flip my lid."

"You play with me and get it in me, and I'll show you, big man," she breathed, hunching. The voluptuous tremors in her loins drew more hot juice from her cunt. It was swelling out. "But I sure don't like this dry stuff."

He laughed. "Yeah, wet is better. But this is a game the girls want to play." His hand stole down across her ass, and she shuddered. She heard Jessica and Amy giggling in the background.

Maybe a younger man is what I need, she thought dreamily. I'm always lining up those middle-aged smoothies, and I wear them out too soon. Sweet Jesus. His cock feels a foot long! Jessica told me he can keep a bone-on for hours he lets her cum and cum and cum.

Jay smiled, enjoying the fine firm cushion of Martha's big tits on his chest. The purple bikini trimmed in white made her lush figure wildly appealing. She had a narrow waist, superb ass, and legs, and there were no wrinkles on her neck or face. She could have passed for thirty any day. But the best feature was her total sensuality. He had noticed that the first time he had met her, and he had figured then he would never have a chance at her.

Not so! Mother wanted his prick, too. The vibes from her lush, mature body were swelling his cockhead, drawing out more juice. She was trying to bore her nipples through the halter into his chest. Her cunt was nestled tightly to his cock-lump. The soft, warm press of it, her slow, eager incurving, kited his passion. He knew she would be a far-out fuck.

"Ohhh, this is agony!" she panted against his throat. "I haven't done this since I was a young girl."

Jay shuddered. The earlier playings with Jessica and Amy had been a real test of his holding abilities. The ache in his groin was almost unbearable. He hadn't busted a load yet today; he knew he had to finish before long, and Martha was dying for prick.

"We're going to change the rules, Martha," he muttered thickly, steering her toward a wide patio cushion. "Get that bikini off."

Martha swung away from him, her head spinning, her whole crotch one big sensuous ache. She hated to get screwed in front of her daughters, but she was so hungry for his cock she didn't care where she was! Thinking about him on her drive up to Rockford, she had turned on so high she had reached into her panties, spread her thighs, and fingered herself into a delicious orgasm. Now she was going to have the real thing!

She snatched her halter from her swollen tits and slid the purple panties down her thighs. Staring at her body, he yanked his trunks from his hips. The view of his prick, angled high and hard, big-knobbed and ready, drew a moan from her throat. When Jessica had hunched and strained to a climax against his lump, she had really stiffened his meat.

Legs wobbly, Martha sank down on the patio cushion, her thighs open wide. Her cunt was a swollen mound of flesh, the gash in the center already showing the pinkness of her inner labia.

She heard excited cries from her daughters, but nothing mattered now except that huge pillar of cockflesh and his big, hairy drivers. God, what a man!

Jessica stared and shivered as Jay sank down between her mother's shaven, spread-apart thighs. She could understand Martha's hunger, her need for cock. She was a ripe, mature woman. Rubbing her pussy on him wasn't enough! She had never seen her mother's breasts so expanded. They were dark mountains of flesh, long-nippled, swollen with her passion, rising straight up, waiting for his mouth. Jay positioned himself, his back arched, knees far apart.

Martha's legs swung toward her chin, her hips raised, and

suddenly his big prickhead was oozing into her flesh. It sank slowly out of sight.

"Ughh!" she cried fiercely. "Jesus!" Her hips jerked upward, her head turned back. His mouth came down to a tit-peak, and the dark spire of flesh went between his lips. He bucked into her cunt and let it soak.

Ohhhh, God! Martha thought, her cock-stuffed vagina starting to convulse on his meat. I was ready to cum half an hour ago when I saw him dancing with Jessica, and now my cunt is finally making the scene! What a prick! That big apple is trying to snug into my womb! Nobody has reached that far for ages! Ohhh, shit! I'm busting my fun!

The heavenly pulsing of her cumjoy racked her whole pelvis! Her cunt was clamping convulsively around his cock, her anus was tightening, and her nipple in his mouth was quivering, expanding. One big hunch, and she was getting her goodies! She screamed as the wild pounding of her joy matched the fury of her tightening cunt. She hadn't had such a big, hard, good cum for years! Every nerve in her crotch was exploding! Her clit was tensing and throbbing, her legs jerking, her tits heaving.

Suddenly he began to fuck! He was drawing way out and then slamming his big cock in hard! His head raised from her tits, his face twisted, his meat tensed, and she knew he was going to cum! Her cuntal muscles knew it; every quivery zone of her body knew it! He was getting ready to spray her hungry cunt with his jism!

Hump, hump, hump! Every delectable stroke heightened her thrall. She was getting those good, hard, deep jabs a real woman just had to have. His groan of pleasure on each drive, as her cunt clenched around his cock, sent more waves of thrills through her loins. A juicy slapping of his drawn-up nuts on her wet, flushed labia soared her pleasure higher, higher!

But he wasn't rushing; he was giving her those delicious thrusts, then waiting. Then, three more thrusts. Ohhh, he knew how to fuck! Again his cockhead was jamming at the opening of her womb. She knew when he went off, he would drive his glans against her cervix and gush the jism deep!

Sonofabitch! Jay thought, stroking hard again. This is the best cunt I ever had! The way it tightens on my dong is fantastic! She's had a cockhead right up to the opening of her womb before it's waiting for my shot. An Indian girl I screwed in Montana was the only one who ever clamped down hard enough to suck the juice right out of my balls. When she went off, I thought she was going to squeeze my glans clear in two. Now, I'm going to have that sensation again. Martha really knows how to fuck! Her daughters need lessons from their mother!

Easy now. Don't blow your wad yet. Give her a real fine fuck, and you'll get more of it, man. He drew way out and jolted in deep again.

He rested, nuzzling her swollen tits, feeling that wild, sweet twitching of her educated cunt.

"Ohhhh, Jesus, that's good!" she panted.

"Terrific cunt," he breathed, every nerve alive to her sensuality.

"Oh, God! It's yours any time you want it!"

Thrust, thrust, thrust! The clinging heat of her cunny, the

trembling of her whole body, the juicy tightening of her labia on his cum-ready prick and tautened nuts began to draw his need. The next time he got to her, he would take more time, but this time, he had saved his shot as long as he ever had. He drove deep again, his cock flexed, and she uttered a fierce moan. She knew the signals she was going to get his load in a few seconds.

Her face contorted, she arched her cunt just a little higher, and it tightened on his meat. He went into his short, bull hunches.

Martha spread her thighs even farther, feeling the extra hardness of his sliding prick, knowing this was the big moment! Her nerves screamed for release. She had held her orgasm until he was ready, and now the sweet shivers of her cunt achieved a stronger response. Her cuntal membranes were clenching, tightening, almost clamping his cock! Her daughters didn't exist now. Nothing mattered except the hot, slippery plunges of his beautiful cock!

The honeyed thrills shot from her nipples, from along her trembling thighs, from her arms and lips and anus. They converged in her loins and launched out to the tip of her tensing clitoris. She shouted! Her cunt was starting its sucking, convulsive trip!

He knew it, and his cock plunged faster, faster! He was horsing her cunt, jamming the knob at the puff of her womb, and just as the wild spasming of her pelvis reached the utter summit of activity, he shuddered and cried out and rammed his knob against her cervix!

The heavenly pulsing of his need, the quiver of his expanded knob in her cuntflesh, and the gush of his jism, all rocked her into dreamland. Her cunt went crazy! It was flogging his cock, the hard spasms reaching from her pelvis to every zone of her body. The thrills lasted and lasted, bathing her with feathery fingers, sating the lust that had gripped her ever since she had first seen him.

* * *

"Mom, you sure yelled your head off!" Jessica giggled, glancing across at her mother, who was sprawled with her thighs apart in a deep chair in the cabin living room.

They had moved inside and were having fresh highballs. Amy sat beside Jay on a sofa. Jessica was in another chair facing the couch. They were all naked, they had all visited the restroom, and Jessica was ready for more fun. So were Martha and Amy. However, it was Amy's turn for goodies.

"When it's real good, I have to yell, honey," Martha laughed, squirming her ass in the chair.

"Aren't we awful?" Amy exclaimed, gazing down at Jay's big, rigid cock. "This nice thing belongs to Jessica, and we're all enjoying it!"

"Oh, I can't be selfish with my own family!" Jessica giggled. "You're both just as crazy about him as I am." She looked across at Jay. "Go ahead and make her cum, honey. Then it'll be my turn!"

More laughter rose above the pulse of the music. Amy, sitting at Jay's left, reached for his cock and opened her thighs. The highballs were finished, and it was fun time again.

His hand settled on Amy's puffy cunt. She gasped, half-turned, and whispered in his ear. He grinned and nodded.

"Amy wants to orgy, gals," he said. "She wants to spread it around a little."

Jessica trembled, remembering the threesome scene earlier when Jay had eaten her cunt for the very first time. Martha sat up straight in her chair, a wide smile on her thick, sensual lips.

"I never went that route, but I'm ready!" she gurgled.

"Oh, it's fun, Mom!" Amy giggled, hunching on his hand. "I saw this in a movie one time, and it was right on!"

* * *

Alexa Daniels spread her thighs farther apart and felt more juice leaking from her cunt. She was resting on her ass on Melanie Welch's bed, her tits swollen from recent kissing, her clit aching for tongue.

Melanie had dropped by the Stern Insurance Company office two days earlier looking for Jay Romero. She had been madder than hell, but the moment she had fastened her eyes on Alexa, her mood changed fast.

They'd had lunch together, had become acquainted, and now Melanie was going to get what she had been after all the time Alexa's cunt. They had gone to an X-rated movie earlier, had downed two martinis apiece afterward, and then had started playing around the moment they entered Melanie's big, luxurious home.

Fuck Jessica and that big-pricked animal, Alexa thought. I like pussy better, anyway. Melanie has been around, she'll know what to do with a hot, eager cunt. At the theater, she got a finger in me, and now I'm going to have her tongue. In a few days, we're going south together, out of this crummy, square burg.

"That's nice looking pussy, honey," Melanie breathed, sliding her hands under Alexa's ass, her head lowering. Her tongue came out and wiggled. A finger played along Alexa's anal crevice. "I'm going to bring you off good and hard."

"Well, get your tongue in there, honey," Alexa breathed. "It's all ready. Then I'm going to eat you."

* * *

Jessica angled her long thighs open and watched Jay crawl forward, his big cock hard and ready for her cock-hungry cunt. She had him to herself, at last! Oh, it had been wild fun doing all the orgy things Amy had dreamed up, like playing leap-frog on his prick, watching him eat Martha while Amy bounced out her shot, feeling his tongue back in her twitchy cunt again, but this was really going to be much better!

Amy and Martha had gone to Martha's cabin. It was past midnight, and as his bride, she did deserve some privacy with her strong, handsome lover. And this time, she was underneath. She knew what that meant he was going to cum in her pussy!

"Am I still number one, honey?" she breathed, arching her crotch higher.

"Hell, you know that, beautiful," he smiled. "Martha got that first load, but this one is all yours."

"Ohhhh, God!" she panted, watching his knob lower toward her uptilted, aching cunny. "Make me cum lots of times!"

Gazing down between her swollen breasts, she watched his wet, huge knob touch her cunt and begin to spread the tender labia. The sweet burn of his flesh, the sensuous yield of her cunt around his glans, had never been more heavenly!

"Ohh, Mmmm!" she panted. She caught her legs with her hands and drew them far forward, the way Martha had positioned herself for his prick.

"Great!" he muttered, squeezing more of his prick in her shivery cunt. As it sank deep, sliding on her clitoris, she stretched cuntal depths tightened. She wasn't even telling her pussy to respond, it was happening involuntarily! He trembled, his cock tensed, his knob pushed at her depths, and her vagina constricted again!

She whimpered. Her nipples stiffened, and her clit began to pulse. The honey of her need shot along her legs, her prick-filled cunt twitched and shivered, her anus puckered, and suddenly, she was rocking her ass up, up, up! The hot pounding of joy was tearing her crotch, heaving her whole pelvis. She screamed!

I'm dimming for him again! she thought wildly. I'm blowing harder than I ever did in my whole life! One jab of his cock did it. Ohh, Ohh, Ohhhh! I'm probably not as hot as Martha, and I have a lot to learn, but he does love my cunt! He likes my long legs and my pointy titties, and my hungry mouth. He knows I need more cock than Amy or Martha. I went without it for years. When he goes home to Los Angeles, I'm going with him. Amy and Martha can come and visit. We'll have more swinging parties, but I'll get more loving than they will!

He's all mine. His huge prick just fits in my cunt, and whenever he wants a little or a lot, he can have it, day or night! This is where it's at! Ohhh, I'm cumming again! Very tall girls can have fun, after all! Ohhhh, sweet Jesus! It isn't my pussy anymore; it belongs to him! It's telling him right now, now, ohh, Now, Now, Now!

The wild, sweet convulsions and churnings of her cunt whirled her clear out of sight.

THE END

Yesteryear's Stories Reflected Today
Yabot AB
www.yabot.se

www.ingramcontent.com/pod-product-compliance
Lightning Source LLC
LaVergne TN
LVHW020054210726

843507LV00016B/2266